"You seen that feller that r____
fered with by the big mars____

The cowboys shook the____ ____ ____ were struggling
not to laugh. Festus knew when he was being made a fool
of and it rubbed him sore. "You'll tell me where he is, you
grinnin' baboon, or I'll arrest you instead!"

The big, handsome Texan stopped smiling and raised his
eyebrows in surprise. "Well, Shorty, that would be a terrible
idea."

"Oh yeah?"

"Yeah."

"Why?"

"'Cause I'd have to feed you your shiny tin badge and I
expect that it would go down hard, what with them sharp,
shiny tin points."

Festus took about three choppy strides forward and
brought his pistol down hard across the top of the cowboy's
hat. The handsome Texan's eyes rolled up into his head like
a pair of marbles and he folded to the sawdust.

"Where is the feller that got Matthew's leg busted?" he
asked as he took a bead on the protester's face. "And I
promise you that Deputy Festus Haggen ain't a-goin' to ask
you any more times."

Berkley Boulevard titles by Gary McCarthy

GUNSMOKE
GUNSMOKE: DEAD MAN'S WITNESS
GUNSMOKE: MARSHAL FESTUS

GUNSMOKE™
MARSHAL FESTUS

A NOVEL BY
GARY McCARTHY

*Based on the radio and television series
created by John Meston*

BERKLEY BOULEVARD BOOKS, NEW YORK

GUNSMOKE: MARSHAL FESTUS

A Berkley Boulevard Book / published by arrangement with Viacom Consumer Products, Inc.

PRINTING HISTORY
Berkley Boulevard edition / July 1999

All rights reserved.
Copyright © 1999 by CBS, Inc.
Cover design by Steven Ferlauto.
Cover art by Hankins and Tegenberg/Bill Dodge.
This book may not be reproduced in whole or in part,
by mimeograph or any other means, without permission.
For information address: The Berkley Publishing Group,
a division of Penguin Putnam Inc.,
375 Hudson Street, New York, New York 10014.

The Penguin Putnam Inc. World Wide Web site address is
http://www.penguinputnam.com

ISBN: 0-425-16974-X

BERKLEY BOULEVARD
Berkley Boulevard Books are published by
The Berkley Publishing Group,
a division of Penguin Putnam Inc.,
375 Hudson Street, New York, New York 10014.
BERKLEY BOULEVARD and its logo
are trademarks belonging to Penguin Putnam Inc.

PRINTED IN THE UNITED STATES OF AMERICA

10 9 8 7 6 5 4 3 2 1

For my dearest Jane

CHAPTER

1

"Marshal Dillon, you'd better get out here fast!" a man cried after sticking his head through the office doorway. "There's a cowboy out here that is causin' real trouble!"

Matt jumped up from his desk. "What . . ."

But the intruder was already gone, so Matt hurried outside to see a drunken Texas cowboy punishing a bucking horse. With a half-empty bottle and his reins clenched in one fist and a quirt in the other, the cowboy made quite a spectacle as his equally drunken friends cheered his ride. The trouble was, the horse was a menace and was endangering other folks.

"Stop that right now, or you're under arrest!" Matt shouted, moving onto Front Street as wagons and other riders tried to get out of his and the bucking horse's paths.

But the bronc rider was too drunk to take a warning. Too drunk, that is, until Matt drew his six-gun and emptied a round into the sky. *That* sure caught the Texan's attention. But instead of dropping his whiskey and grabbing leather to bring the bronc under control, the rider yanked out his own gun and began firing into the sky and shouting, "Yippee!"

Matt could see that it was useless to reason with the cowboy, and when the bronc slammed into a passing carriage, he was intent on grabbing its bit and forcing it to a standstill. And he'd have succeeded, too, except that the cowboy was so drunk he fell off the horse, which shied and crashed into a water trough, turning it over and spilling its contents into the dust. Terrified, the beast whirled and started to run. Now the cowboy realized that he was about to be dragged and that this prank could cost him his life.

Matt was the only man quick thinking and sober enough to grab the bronc's reins. He dug his heels into the hard-packed earth and braced his legs to pull the horse's neck around, but the animal was so crazed it fought him, rearing and striking. Matt tore the cowboy's boot free but the horse slammed into him, lost its footing, and went down kicking. Matt felt a stab of intense pain in his lower left leg and collapsed, barely avoiding a flying hoof in the face. The horse shook itself, climbed to its feet, and raced out of Dodge City, heading south.

Matt was nearly paralyzed with pain. The drunken Texan was covered with blood but apparently had not suffered any serious injuries since he was able to crawl over to Matt's side and ask, "You okay, Marshal?"

"No! I . . ." Matt grimaced, nearly overcome with nausea. His leg was bent at a peculiar angle, but there was no blood to indicate that the bone had pierced his flesh. "Someone get Doc Adams! Hurry!"

A half-dozen cowboys scattered like quail in search of the doctor; Matt gritted his teeth and tried not to lose consciousness.

"Matt!"

He opened his eyes to see a crowd of the townspeople. There were storekeeper Lathrop; the busybody Halligan; the town's freight agent, Nathan Burke; their crusty old telegrapher, Barney; and Percy Crump, the undertaker, who was always one of the first to arrive after the gunshots died.

Matt's focus quickly settled on Kitty and Festus, who were kneeling by his side, expressions pale and grim. Festus said, "Doc had to leave town this morning in his buggy to help deliver Mrs. Johnson's baby."

"I need to get off the street. Help me up."

"Are you sure you ought to move?"

"Yeah," Matt grated. "I'm sure. My leg is broken, but I think the rest of me is still in one piece. Come on, help me up."

"I'll help, too," Kitty said. "Matt, you're coming over to my place until Doc says otherwise."

"I'm in no shape to argue."

"Good!" Kitty said with her lips pursed tightly in worry. "That's a first."

The pain was so intense that Matt didn't think he could make it to the Long Branch Saloon, but he did, somehow. Kitty ordered Festus and several others to help carry him upstairs to her private quarters. Matt was plenty familiar with Kitty's place and figured he'd be comfortable.

"Place him on the bed," Kitty ordered. "Easy, now!"

Matt could feel the sweat beading on his forehead as they gently laid him down. "Festus?"

"Yeah?"

"Arrest that drunken Texas cowboy. Charge him with being drunk and disorderly and fine both him and his friends five dollars each. That ought to about pay Doc for what he's going to do to me."

"I sure will, Matthew! Anything else?"

"Not that I can think of."

"Well, Festus," Kitty interrupted, "after you do that you ought to ride out to the Johnson place and see how Doc is coming with that delivery. Tell him Matt is in a lot of pain. Maybe he can give you something to bring back quick."

"Yes, ma'am! I'll do that." Festus shooed the others out of Kitty's room, then turned to look back. "Matthew,

I sure am sorry about this. You oughta let that fool get dragged to death."

"Nobody deserves to die that way," Matt replied.

"Well, maybe not, but . . . well, how we goin' to get along without you?"

"You'll just have to pick up the slack for a while," Matt told his only full-time deputy. "I know that you are up to the task."

Festus gulped, his prominent Adam's apple bobbing up and down. As usual, his face was covered with a three-day stubble and his clothes were dirty and wrinkled. He pulled nervously on his battered old Stetson and whined, "I'll sure try to uphold your office, Matthew, but you know that—"

Kitty had heard more than enough. "Go on, Festus! Arrest them fools, take their money, and then go find Doc! Could be that Mrs. Johnson isn't even going to have that baby today and Doc is just sitting around smoking and sipping her husband's corn liquor! Hurry, now!"

"Yes, ma'am!"

Festus scuttled out the door and Kitty slammed it shut.

"Don't you think maybe you were a bit hard on him?" Matt asked.

"No! Festus needs to learn to take charge. Why, if you hadn't given him orders, he'd probably have just sat around here fretting and moaning for a week or two. Matthew, sometimes—"

"Kitty," Matt interrupted, "you know that Festus is a good man in a fight. He's loyal and brave. Never mind that he doesn't seem too eager or willing to take charge. That's my job anyway."

"Fine," Kitty said, "but you are going to be laid up for a good long while. So who is going to handle the next crisis in Dodge?"

"Festus will do fine," Matt replied without a moment's hesitation.

"Do you really believe that?"

"I sure do."

4

Kitty retrieved a pair of scissors. She cut Matt's left pant leg and stared at the purplish-colored flesh and the knob that showed where the shinbone had broken. Her lower lip trembled and tears glistened in her lovely green eyes. "Oh, Matt, it looks just awful."

"Could be far worse if the bone had splintered through. I consider myself lucky."

"Some luck." Kitty sighed. "Matt, I'm no doctor, but I can say without guessing that your leg is badly broken."

"I already knew that."

"Well," Kitty said, "you are going to be out of commission for a good long while."

"You make it sound pretty bad."

"Take a look for yourself."

Matt raised his head from the pillow and stared down at his discolored and rapidly swelling leg. Lips compressed tightly in pain and discouragement, he fell back and closed his eyes.

"I'm so sorry," Kitty said. "But at least I'll have you where I want you for a couple of months or more."

"Maybe Festus was right," he said, more to himself than to Kitty.

"About what?"

"About letting that cowboy get dragged to death."

"Don't be ridiculous! We both know you couldn't have allowed that to happen. That is not the way you are made, Marshal Dillon."

Matt was trying to think of a reply, but just then Festus banged on the door. "Matthew, I got to ask you a question!"

"Come on in!"

Festus entered, swept off his hat, and rolled the brim nervously in his dirty hands. "I . . . I forgot something."

"What?"

"Well, I forgot if you wanted me to arrest *all* them cowboys or just the one that you saved."

"Just the one. But fine him ten dollars and his friends five each."

5

"Why, sure! But what if they all went into the saloon? Matthew, I don't know which ones were hootin' and hollerin' and ought to be fined. And you know that every last one of 'em will say he wasn't out there and—"

"Festus?"

"Yes, sir?"

"Just fine the fella that was riding his bucking horse. Fine him twenty dollars instead of ten."

"And if he ain't got it, should I keep him locked up in jail?"

"I think you should," Matt said patiently, although the throbbing pain in his leg was killing him.

"Okay," Festus said, nodding and casting a toothy smile at Miss Kitty. "Don't you worry about a thing, Matthew. Old Festus is gonna take care of things."

"I know that."

"Go on!" Kitty cried with exasperation. "Arrest that man and find Doc!"

"I'm as good as gone," Festus assured her. "As good as gone."

He tripped on his way out the door, and when it closed, Kitty shook her head. "Lord help us poor folks in Dodge City while he's the law."

Matt wanted laudanum, but he figured whiskey would do until then. "Bring me a bottle, Kitty. Bring the strongest stuff you have at the bar. And don't worry so much about Festus."

"I can't help it, and I'm not worried about myself or anything but about *him*. Matt, he's liable to get into something over his head and get killed." ·

"Festus is a crack shot, an expert tracker, and he's a lot smarter than he looks. I wouldn't have hired him after Chester left if I didn't think he could do the job."

"Well," Kitty said, "I just hope he doesn't forget what he is supposed to do and that Doc Adams returns soon. You must be feeling terrible."

"I've had better days," Matt told her. "Now please get that whiskey."

When Kitty left and he was finally alone, Matt sat up on the bed and reexamined his broken leg. He knew that there were two bones and that they might both be fractured. But despite the rapid swelling and discoloration, he still figured he was lucky. Doc called this a simple fracture, while a compound fracture was the term he used when you could see splintered bone and knew that infection was going to be a major problem, one that often forced amputation.

I'm one lucky fella, Matt told himself again before he lay back down and closed his eyes. *I got a good doctor coming, a beautiful woman that's going to take care of me like I was a complete invalid, and a deputy who has more try in him than any five other men. Festus won't let me down and neither will anyone else.*

Yep, I'm real lucky.

It seemed to take a long time for Kitty to return with the whiskey, and Matt's huge fists were clenched when he reached for the full water glass she extended.

"Drink this and you might not remember anything for the next few hours."

"That strong?"

"You be the judge," Kitty replied.

Matt drank the whiskey in a few jolting gasps. "Fer crying out loud!" he choked. "What is in this stuff?"

"Turpentine and rattlesnake poison would be my best guess," Kitty said, refilling the glass and helping herself to a generous portion. "I only use it in emergencies and this is definitely an emergency."

"I might feel worse than I do right now if I drink any more," Matt told her.

Kitty winked and sipped more whiskey. "Well," she said, "if *my* leg looked even half as bad as *your* leg, I'd take my chances and drink up all of this that I could stand."

Matt nodded and reached for the bottle. He upended it and felt the fiery liquor burn his gullet like a torch and hit his stomach like a fist.

"Whew!" he gasped. "That one tasted a little better."

"You'll get used to it," Kitty promised as she stretched out beside him.

"What are you doing?" he asked.

"I'm gonna lie here and help you finish this bottle. Then maybe we can take a nap."

"I never take naps."

"Well, you should," Kitty told him. "Festus takes them. Doc takes them, and so do I. You're not so young anymore that you couldn't stand to gain by taking an afternoon snooze either."

"Too much to do."

"Not now. Not tomorrow and not for a couple of months, if I am right about what Doc is going to prescribe for that broken leg of yours." Kitty giggled, indicating that the whiskey might already be affecting her normally good senses. "Matt, you need to learn to relax and enjoy life. You work too hard and you take things too seriously."

"Give me that bottle," he growled, feeling the pain diminish. "I'm going to drink it dry."

"That's the spirit!" Kitty gracefully bounced off the bed to her feet and started for the door.

"Hey, where are you going?"

"I'm going to get another bottle of Mule Pucker."

"That's what it's called?"

"Yep. They say that if you give it to a mule, it will make him bray and pucker."

"Huh," Matt grunted, drinking again and then opening his mouth and letting the fumes burn the air. "For gawd-sake, Kitty, don't light a candle in here or we're goners for certain!"

Kitty giggled some more and then disappeared. Matt took another long series of lightning jolts of Mule Pucker and closed his eyes. After that, he didn't remember anything.

CHAPTER

2

The world seemed to rest heavily on Festus Haggen's troubled shoulders as he headed back down to the street to find and arrest the battered cowboy whose life Matthew had just saved. He wasn't so much concerned about his own hide as he was worried about upholding Marshal Dillon's high standards and expectations. Matt was big, smart, and tough, and Festus considered himself none of those things, although he was no quitter and had won a few more scrapes than he'd lost.

He'd come out of the hill country back east, where things were different and people were simple. Not that they were stupid or anything, but they tended to see things as either right or wrong, black or white. It had taken Festus quite a while to realize that there were a lot of grays in this world, meaning that you had to consider many different facts before determining whether a man was good or bad, guilty or innocent. Fortunately, there was Marshal Dillon and Judge Brooker to lean on pretty heavy . . . and there was the law.

Festus loved the law. It was simple and straightforward. All the rules governing people were spelled out in black-and-white so that you knew without question whether someone committed a crime or not. Now, bucking out a bronc in the middle of Front Street at high noon in August was definitely a crime because it endangered lives. So finding the battered Texas cowboy and arresting him was not a problem in Festus's mind. However, fining the cowboy twenty dollars to cover Matthew's doctor's expenses was not exactly legal. On the other hand, Festus knew that old Judge Brooker, once he heard all the facts and saw how bad a shape it caused Matthew to be in now, would certainly fine the cowboy at least twenty dollars.

Well, orders were orders, Festus thought as he angled across the street toward the Alhambra Saloon, where the last of the Texans who'd driven cattle up the long trail were usually gathered. Just a few weeks ago the streets of Dodge City had been filled with boisterous cowboys, all itching to spend the last of their trail-drive wages before heading back down to Texas. But now most of the longhorn cattle had been sold, shipped east on the railroad, and the cowboys had gone home mostly busted, but vowing to return the next spring and raise a ruckus again in Dodge, Wichita, and all the other Kansas trail towns. Good thing that it was late August and not early June, when the onslaught typically began.

The Alhambra wasn't real busy, but the half-dozen or so Texans inside made it sound like there was one heck of a big crowd. They were hollerin', cussin', and laughin' just as if nothing had happened out on Front Street less than fifteen minutes earlier.

Festus, realizing he was not very impressive looking, straightened his deputy badge, pushed out his chest, and cleared his throat loudly in order to attract their attention. But he got no response. The Texans were either ignoring him or they didn't even realize that the law of Dodge City had just arrived.

"All you Texas fellers listen up to me a minute," he shouted over the din.

They kept ignoring him, so Festus dragged out his six-gun, intending to unload a round into the ceiling. But then he remembered Matthew telling him that the saloon owners hated that because it meant patching a hole when it rained. That being the case, Festus pointed his gun downward and fired into the floor. The result was better than he'd hoped. The cowboys froze, then spun around to regard him with more annoyance than interest.

"Now listen up, you boys!" Festus called. "One of your friends, and I don't see him just now, tried to ride a buckin' horse in this here street outside. I reckon you saw the sad results of that foolishness and know that Marshal Dillon got his leg broke and your friend nearly got his hide peeled all off by a draggin'."

A tall, handsome young cowboy leaned back against the bar top and drawled, "Mister, you look a little short in the pants to be wearing that badge. Why don't you tell us something that we *don't* know."

Festus bristled. "All right, I will! Your friend, the fool, is under arrest for endangerin' the public and gettin' Matthew's leg busted. Now where is he?"

"Beats me."

The cowboy was grinning when he turned first to his left then to his right, asking his friends, "You seen that feller that rode the bucker until he was interfered with by the big marshal?"

The cowboys shook their heads. Most were struggling not to laugh. Festus knew when he was being made a fool of and it rubbed him sore. "You'll tell me where he is, you grinnin' baboon, or I'll arrest you instead!"

The big, handsome Texan stopped smiling and raised his eyebrows in surprise. "Well, Shorty, that would be a terrible idea."

"Oh yeah?"

"Yeah."

"Why?"

" 'Cause I'd have to feed you your shiny tin badge and I expect that it would go down hard, what with them sharp, shiny tin points."

The crowd of Texans found this remark to be hilarious. They threw back their heads and brayed at the chandeliers like a bunch of coyotes. They would have howled even longer, except that Festus took about three choppy strides forward and brought his pistol down hard across the top of the cowboy's hat, putting a deep new crease in its fancy crown. The handsome Texan's eyes rolled up into his head like a pair of marbles and he folded to the sawdust.

Someone cussed and then Festus had that man in his gun sights; the protester lost both his voice and his nerve. Festus knew that if they were all drunk enough to go for their guns, he was a sure dead man, but he was just damned mad enough to take that risk.

"Where is the feller that got Matthew's leg busted?" he asked as he took a bead on the protester's face. "And I promise you that Deputy Festus Haggen ain't a-goin' to ask you any more times."

"He's out back in a crib with Skinny Sally," the cowboy stammered, raising his now shaking hands. "We all chipped in money to pay her to take care of him after we leave."

"What's his name?"

"George. George Apple."

"Since he couldn't pay old Skinny Sally, I guess that means that George is broke, huh?"

"Dead broke."

Festus thought about this for a long moment or two, then made his decision. "Well, Matthew's leg is bad broke and Doc needs to get paid. So you boys pass the hat for Matthew's doctorin' expenses."

"Why should we do that!" wailed the cowboy who was staring down the muzzle of Festus's gun barrel.

"You're lookin' at the reason, mister."

"You can't fine us! We ain't done nothing wrong!"

"Yes, you did."

"What?"

Festus had to think fast. "Well," he struggled, "you . . . you just refused to give information to a law officer and it's going to cost you boys at least twenty dollars."

"Twenty dollars, we won't—"

Whatever the cowboy had been about to say was forgotten as Festus took a step forward and poked his barrel between the man's bloodshot eyes.

"You gonna pass the hat or pass over into the next world?" Festus asked solemnly.

"Jaysus, don't shoot, Deputy!" the cowboy said, whipping his own hat from his head and reaching for his pocket. "We'll pass the hat!"

It was done, and done quickly. Festus counted the money with one eye on the Texans; there was a little over twenty dollars, so he thanked the cowboys and headed out to see George Apple and Skinny Sally.

They were in the little alley crib that Sally stayed in. When Festus opened the door and saw poor George Apple, he forgot about making an arrest because the drunken cowboy was a scabby, bleeding mess.

"Festus, what do you want!" the woman demanded.

"I sorta had it in mind to arrest him."

"He's suffered enough," Sally hissed. "George ain't got any hide left on his backside and his face is nearly all scraped off."

Festus could see that Sally was telling the gospel truth. "Miss Sally," he said, taking off his hat, "the cowboys inside gave you some money to take care of George Apple while he heals. If you run out, come see me and we'll collect some more. That man sure looks raw . . . sorta like a peeled grape."

George must have heard that because one of his eyes opened and he moaned. Sally had started to undress and wash him, but Festus could see that it was going to be a terrible chore.

"Wait until he sobers up and really starts yelling," Sally bitterly replied. "I got a feeling that I'm going to earn every cent of my doctorin' money."

"Well, it might do you good to be an angel of kindness and mercy instead of a soiled, fallen dove," Festus opined.

"You got no right to call me 'soiled,' Deputy Haggen! Why, look at yourself in the mirror . . . if you dare. You're as filthy, and you smell!"

Festus took a faltering backward step, recovered his dignity, and shouted, "Sally, I'll have you know that I'm acting town marshal until Matthew gets back on his feet!"

"You ain't no marshal! You're just a dirty deputy, as randy and rank as any billy goat! You might wear the marshal's badge, but nobody will take you serious. Now git!"

Festus was wounded, deeply wounded. He snorted through both nostrils and headed up the alley, feeling angry and shamed. He would find his horse, get Doc, then he would take a look at himself in the mirror just to remind himself that he wasn't such a bad-looking fella. Maybe he did need to bathe now and then and change his clothes more often. And shave every two instead of every three days. But appearances did not take the measure of any man. Why, that tall, handsome young Texan in the saloon had just learned this lesson the hard way, hadn't he?

When he reached the Johnson homestead later that afternoon after a hard ride, Doc was sitting on the porch smoking his pipe and sipping whiskey, just as Kitty had expected.

"Festus, you come all the way out here just to share a little whiskey with me on this porch?"

"No, Doc!" Festus was hot and as sweaty as his horse. He crawled out of his saddle and wiped his face with his sleeve. "Matthew has been hurt."

Dr. Galen Adams came to his feet, brow furrowing. "What happened?"

"There was a drunken cowboy and he was about to get dragged to death in the street. Matthew ran out and saved his fool hide, but he got his leg broke real bad."

"Compound fracture?"

"Huh?"

Doc was not a man of great patience and now he shouted, "Did the bone push through his skin!"

"No, sir, at least not that it showed none."

"Thank God!" Doc downed his whiskey and knocked the bowl of his pipe clean against the nearest porch post. "I got Mrs. Johnson here and she's started her labor. I can't leave her now."

"Well, Doc, you got to help Matthew 'cause he's in a whole lot of hurt!"

"I've got something in my bag that will help. You take it to Matt and tell him I'll be along just as soon as I can. Tell him not to move."

"Miss Kitty won't let him. She's given him some Mule Pucker whiskey. You ever tried that, Doc?"

He almost smiled. "I'm afraid that I have and that information changes the dosage of the laudanum that I'll be prescribing."

Festus was about to say more, but just then he heard Mrs. Johnson cry out in pain. "Well, I'll be leavin' with that there medicine, Doc."

Doc gave him a dose of laudanum with instructions. "Remember to tell Matt not to move. I'll be in to set that break just as fast as I can get this baby delivered and Mrs. Johnson comfortable."

"Thank you, Doc!"

"What's Matt going to do about getting someone to replace him? He'll have to stay off his feet for quite a while, you know."

"I know. He . . . well, he wants me to be marshal until he can recover."

15

"You?"

"Well, yes, sir! I'm his only deputy, ain't I?"

"Sure, but I thought he might want to wire some of the other towns and—"

"Maybe he will when he thinks it out," Festus allowed. "He's in a lot of pain and maybe not thinking so clear."

Doc reached out and put a hand on Festus's shoulder. "Listen, I think Matt Dillon was *born* talking straight and thinking clear. And I think he is right to pick you to wear his badge for a while."

"You do?"

"Sure! I just said that I did, didn't I?"

"Yes, sir."

"You'll be all right, Festus. You'll do just fine."

"Thanks, Doc. I appreciate you sayin' that."

"Well, before we start gettin' misty-eyed," Doc said cryptically, "you'd best get back to town with that medicine."

"I sure aim to do that!"

Festus remounted and galloped off back to Dodge City. It was ten miles but it had seemed like a hundred on his way out to find Doc. It was going to seem like another hundred on the return trip.

Only good thing was, the riding kept his mind off all the new responsibilities that he was going to have to handle. That, and the terrible things that Skinny Sally had said about him in the alley.

CHAPTER

3

"Miss Kitty, how is Matthew doin'?" Festus asked, winded after his long ride and short sprint through her Long Branch Saloon.

"He's a little drunk but feeling a whole lot better." Kitty smiled loosely. "Matter of fact, we're *both* a little drunk."

"Miss Kitty! I don't know as how that's such a good idea."

"Festus, if your leg was broken as bad as Matt's, you'd think it was a real good idea." She looked past him to the front door. "Where is Doc?"

"He's a-comin' just as soon as he can deliver Mrs. Johnson's baby."

"But that could take hours!"

"I reckon," Festus said. "Doc don't have no choice but to wait."

"I'm tempted to set that leg myself," Kitty mused aloud. "You know the longer it is before we set the bone, the harder."

"I know, but—"

"Did Doc give you any medicine?"

"Some laudanum."

"Hmm," Kitty mused. "Let's give it to Matt and then, if Doc doesn't come in another hour, we'll try to set the bone ourselves."

"Do you really think we should try that?" Festus asked, looking doubtful. "I mean . . . well, this is real serious."

"Of course it is! But I know from firsthand experience that the muscles of Matt's leg are tightening and that the swelling can only get worse as time passes. Both will make it harder to set the bone properly."

"Yeah, but—"

"No buts about it! Mrs. Johnson is in a fix and Doc can't leave her, but we can't let Matt down at this end, can we?"

"We sure can't, Miss Kitty."

"Give me the laudanum and I'll wake Matt up and tell him we might have to set his leg by ourselves. If he objects, we'll wait for Doc. But he won't because Matt knows I'm right and that the leg has to be set soon or it will become nearly impossible."

"Yes, ma'am." Festus was feeling worse by the minute. "Maybe I should have a whiskey myself."

"Good idea. Tell Sam it is on the house."

Festus gave Kitty the medicine and then went to get himself a shot of courage.

"Where's Doc?" Sam asked after getting Festus's request for a double shot of Mule Pucker.

"Stuck out at the Johnson homestead waiting for Mrs. Johnson to deliver her first baby."

"That's not good news."

Sam was a large, friendly man who had been Kitty's main bartender for several years. He worked hard, kept pretty much to himself, and was well liked by most everyone. "Is it true that you're going to be the new marshal of Dodge City until Matt gets better?"

"I suppose that I am," Festus answered, tossing down the whiskey and clearing his throat. "One more, Sam. After that, I'd best go over to the office to check on things. I'll be back in an hour to see if we can set Matt's broken leg if Doc hasn't returned by then."

"Well now, Festus," Sam replied, shaking his head back and forth. "I don't think you ought to try and mess with a broken bone. I seen bones set by people that didn't know what they were doing. They looked terrible years later. And if you and Miss Kitty set it wrong, you could cripple poor Matt for life."

Festus knew this to be true, but until this very moment he had managed not to think about the consequences of doing a poor job on Matthew. Tossing down his second drink, he cleared his throat and said in a gravelly voice, "Let's hope we don't have to do it."

"If you do, you'll be sorry."

Festus had heard quite enough of that kind of talk and so he headed for the office. He and Matthew had recently nailed a bulletin board up for folks to leave messages just in case both lawmen were out on business. That way, they'd know if there was anything important to do next.

Fortunately, there were no messages on the board. Festus went inside and turned on a lamp because it was just past sundown. He scanned the small office, noticing for the first time how different Matthew's desk was compared with his own. The marshal's desk was tidy while his was littered with papers, a broken bridle, and even an old black powder Army Colt pistol that Festus was cleaning, with the accompanying mess of dirty and solvent-soaked rags.

Festus scowled and then walked over to a mirror that was hanging on the wall. It was a large mirror, big enough to show a man from head to foot. Regarding himself with the same critical eye he'd used on his desk, Festus had to admit that he was a sorry-looking figure. His clothes were baggy, patched, and filthy, while his boots were scuffed and worn nearly off at the heels. All the dust that he'd just collected from his long ride out to the Johnson homestead only helped to hide all the food and grease stains.

No wonder Skinny Sally and all the rest are worried about me taking over while Matthew is down, Festus thought. *I look like some drunk that sleeps under a porch and ain't got money nor good sense. How could anyone respect a man who looks like me?*

Right there and then, Festus resolved to improve his slovenly appearance and he'd do it first thing tomorrow. He could certainly afford new duds . . . from hat to boots. Thing of it was, though, his old boots felt good, his hat still fit and kept the sun off'n the back of his neck and front of his face. His shirt might be a sad affair, but it covered him just fine and his pants were as comfortable as a pair of old long johns. And who needed a leather belt and buckle when you wore a gun belt over the top of it?

Festus wrestled with both sides of the argument for changing his appearance, realizing finally that, at the root of it, he was sloppy because he really hated to spend money. He'd come from a real hardscrabble life in the far hills, where two bits was a lot of money and where a family rarely saw cash. His people had raised what they'd eaten and traded for what they couldn't raise to fill out the rest of their needs. Cash money came hard and Festus had saved most of his deputy's wages in a bean can under his floorboards until Matthew insisted he use the bank. Having money in the bank—more than seven hundred dollars now—gave Festus immense pride. And he wasn't no cheapskate, either. Why, whenever his poor kinfolks came to Dodge City, he paid their bills and he was known to be a soft touch, always willing to help out some poor fella down on his luck. Money spent to help others was money better spent than on fancy clothes that he didn't really need.

"Stop thinkin' like that," he ordered himself out loud. "If you're a-goin' to wear Marshal Dillon's badge even for one minute out there on the town, you've got to do it to make *him* proud. Spend twenty . . . no, you can't do it all for no twenty dollars. Why, a decent pair of boots alone will cost you that much. And a good Stetson hat will cost nearly as much. You'll need more than one shirt and pair of pants, too."

Festus sighed and shook his head at his disreputable image. "Before the clothes, you'll need to get a bath, haircut, and shave. No use in puttin' your own smelly self in new clothes, or they'll soon smell bad, too."

The decision to go ahead and change the way he dressed did not bring Festus any joy since he knew this was all going to add up to around a hundred dollars. He also figured to start wearing a belt and maybe even new socks in his new boots. At least he would not have to purchase a new coat, since Matthew would be back to work before the cold autumn winds arrived.

"Deputy Haggen?"

He turned to see the town banker standing in the door. Feeling self-conscious at being caught staring at himself in the mirror, Festus struggled to smile. "Evening, Mr. Brodkin. What can I do for you?"

"You can tell me what is going on around here!"

Brodkin was not a pleasant man to deal with. Pompous and aware of his importance to Dodge City as the head of its main bank, he was quick to give his opinion and set people to his way of thinking.

"You mean about Matthew?"

"Of course! I was out of town most of today and just returned. What happened to Dillon?"

Festus explained in as few words as he could. Wanting to put the best light possible on things, he ended up saying, "But you don't have to worry, sir. Matthew is going to be just fine."

"I know that! After all, he broke his leg, not his neck. But what about my town? Who is going to be in charge?"

Unable to resist taking another quick glance at his

image in the mirror before giving his reply, Festus was ashamed to say, "I am, sir."

"You?" Brodkin's jaw dropped. "You!"

"Yes, sir."

"Festus, no offense, but we need a real lawman to handle this town. I know that most of the cowboys are gone now, but there are a few dozen left and they're always eager to cause trouble. I'm sure that they know Marshal Dillon is out of commission and they're just itching to hoo-rah this town."

"If they try, they'll be arrested, jailed, and then sent to court for fining, same as usual."

"They will resist arrest and then what will you do?" Brodkin asked. "You're no marshal and never will be. I'm afraid that I'm going to have to call an emergency meeting of the town council tomorrow and begin an immediate search for Dillon's temporary replacement!"

"You do that, sir," Festus said, feeling the hairs on the back of his neck rising. "But right now I ain't got the time to talk anymore. I got to make the rounds real quick then get back over to the Long Branch and see if Doc Adams has returned. And if he hasn't, me and Miss Kitty are going to try and set Matt's leg straight again."

"What!"

"You heard me," Festus grated as he marched over to the door, gently but firmly took Brodkin by the arm, and steered him back outside so he could lock up and get on with his business.

"I meant no offense but . . . man, how long has it been since you took a bath?"

It was almost dark outside, which was a good thing because Festus could feel his face flush with anger. "Good night, sir," he choked as he hitched up his beltless pants and started on his rounds.

"You've also been drinking, haven't you?" Brodkin challenged. "I smelled whiskey on your breath!"

Festus did not trust himself to answer, so he ducked

into the first saloon he came to, wiped his nose on the back of his sleeve, and called, "Everything okay in here tonight?"

"Just fine," the bartender shouted back. "How's the marshal?"

"He's going to be all right."

"Where they gonna find someone to fill his boots?"

Festus wanted to tell them that no man alive could fill Matt Dillon's boots, but that he was going to give it his very best try. But he was afraid that they'd just laugh and make fun of him, so he answered, "I don't know yet for sure."

"Gonna be hard," the bartender lamented with a sad shake of his balding head. "Gonna be darned near impossible."

Festus figured that was true enough, so he nodded in agreement and headed back outside, glad to see that Mr. Brodkin was gone.

One look at Sam and Miss Kitty's faces told Festus that Doc had not yet returned to town. Kitty took his arm and said, "I talked it over with Matt and he agrees that we can't wait any longer to set his leg."

"Did you give him the laudanum?"

"Yes, just as soon as you left. He's feeling no pain."

"That could change quick when we start bendin' and yankin' on that broken bone."

"I know, but we've no choice. Doc would say the same thing. He must be going crazy worrying about what to do. Mrs. Johnson isn't a very strong woman and her husband had to leave for work in Colorado. He's stuck out there until that baby arrives."

"Mr. Johnson should have taken his wife to Colorado with him."

"I know, but that doesn't change things for us . . . or for Matt. We have to reset that leg, Festus. Are you up to it?"

"I guess."

"If you're not," Sam offered, "I'll stand in for you."

"No," Festus told him. "I ought to do it 'cause he's my best friend."

"Suit yourself," the bartender replied, not bothering to hide his relief.

"Come on," Kitty declared, "let's get this over with."

Festus followed Miss Kitty back into her room and found Matt wide-awake. "Festus," he said louder than was necessary, "it's about time you came back. Now, don't worry about a thing. You and Kitty will do fine. Other than a doctor, I can't think of anyone I'd rather have a go at setting my leg."

Matthew's confidence made Festus feel better. He could see that Miss Kitty had everything ready, including a pair of splints. "How we gonna do this?"

Matt answered. "I've broken my leg before and it was set by one man. I'll grab the headboard and hang on while you and Kitty grab the leg and yank it hard. I'm hoping that it'll just sort of pop into place. You'll know when that happens because the leg won't be crooked anymore."

"That's it?" Festus asked.

"That's it, Marshal Haggen."

Festus appreciated Matthew trying to pump up his confidence by calling him "marshal." "All right," he said, taking a deep breath and gently taking hold of Matthew's left ankle, while trying to avoid looking at the hugely swollen and badly discolored leg. "I guess I'm ready."

"What am I supposed to do?" Kitty asked.

"Grab hold of the leg and squeeze it tight. When the bone pops into alignment, you'll feel it, and for gosh sakes tell Festus to stop pulling!"

Festus watched as Matthew grabbed the big oak headboard and clenched his teeth so hard that the cords of his jaw muscles stood out like strips of rawhide. "Here goes, Matthew."

Festus tightened his grip and then he threw his weight and muscle backward in a sudden, violent motion. He heard Matthew roar through his clenched teeth and then Kitty screamed, "Stop!"

Festus let go of the ankle so fast that he crashed over backward. He jumped up and saw that Matthew's face was as pale as a gravestone but that the leg was straight.

"Do you think we got it?"

"I don't know for sure," Kitty whispered, also looking pale and shaken. "But it *feels* right."

Matt was gasping for breath and now he slowly released the headboard, heaved a big sigh, and went limp.

"Good job," he whispered. "I knew you could do it."

Matthew's eyes were closed and his face was covered with cold sweat, but Kitty got a washrag and wiped him dry. Not knowing what else to do or say, Festus tiptoed back to the door and eased down the hallway.

"How'd it go?" Sam asked.

"Whiskey! Mule Pucker, if you got some."

"You look like you could use it."

"I can."

Festus wasn't much of a drinking man, but if he hadn't been carrying the new responsibilities of being town marshal now, he might have gotten drunk this night.

Instead, he had taken three shots of Mule Pucker and headed off to bed down on a cot in the office tonight. Tomorrow, by gawd, he would transform himself into a new and a better man. It would cost him plenty, but he would make Matthew, Kitty, and Doc proud.

He would, by jingo.

CHAPTER

4

"Festus, you want what!" the highly regarded owner of the Centennial Barbershop exclaimed.

Festus glared at the town's best barber and repeated his request. "Mr. Butterworth, I want a haircut, a shave, and then a bath with some of that there lavender soap instead of the lye. How much will it cost?"

Melvin Butterworth was a dapper, impeccably dressed gentleman in his early forties. His Centennial Barbershop didn't cater to the cowboys and rough workingmen; instead he prided himself on keeping the city's more prominent and prosperous members looking well groomed. And so it was that Festus had never had much to do with Butterworth before. However, he did know that Matthew wouldn't have considered going to any other barber in town, so it seemed only right that, as Matthew's replacement, he do the same.

Butterworth smiled condescendingly and replied, "Why don't you just use a knife, scissors, and then jump in the horse trough, Mr. Haggen? That way you could save yourself two dollars and save me a great unpleasantness."

"Two dollars it is, then," Festus said, trying to ignore the snickers he heard from the other waiting customers. "But I can't sit around here waiting for all these folks."

"Why not?"

"Well, sir, in case you hadn't heard, Matthew got his leg broke and he asked me to become the marshal until he's back on his feet."

"Lord help us!" Butterworth cried with mock terror. "The town is doomed!"

Everyone laughed outright then, and Festus got so mad that he stomped his battered boot down hard and shouted, "You can all laugh like a bunch of hyenas! Go ahead, if you want! But if you have trouble, then you'd better not come runnin' to Marshal Festus Haggen, 'cause all I'll do is laugh right back in your stupid faces!"

His outburst quelled the laughter and Butterworth raised his hand for complete silence, saying, "Very well, Marshal Haggen. I've always believed that a man's appearance is a signal of his inner worth. But what good will a haircut and shave do wearing those clothes!"

"I'm a-gonna buy me a whole new set soon as I get cleaned up," Festus answered. "I mean to change my image."

"That would be . . . nice," Butterworth said, tugging on his handlebar mustache. "But you've got quite a lot of work to do besides your appearance."

"Such as!"

"Don't *whine*! Try to speak slowly and enunciate your words properly."

"Huh?"

"Oh, never mind. Just try to speak proper English and"—Butterworth made a face—"and don't wipe your nose on your sleeve. Use a clean handkerchief. Polish your boots."

"I'm a-gonna buy me some new ones with new socks, too."

"Good!" Butterworth smiled. "I will clean you up, but only on the condition that you agree to come here every day for a shave and a bath."

"What!"

"I'm serious," Butterworth told him, looking very serious indeed. "It will do you no good to get respectable today if you revert to your old unclean habits tomorrow. You *must* shave every day and get a haircut every two weeks."

"My gawd, man! You trying to break me, or something!"

"No," Butterworth said, "I'm trying to help you make a permanent change. However, if at the end of one month you do not agree that my services and your own efforts aren't worth the money or the bother, then quit!"

"What if I have to go out of town after an outlaw or something?"

"Then we will, of course, suspend the requirements. What say you, Marshal? Have we a deal?"

"I can't afford to pay you two dollars every other day!"

"One dollar will do after this appointment." Butterworth folded his arms across his narrow chest. "And I believe these gentlemen will be willing to allow you in ahead of them today. Won't you?"

The "gentlemen" were having a real hard time keeping from laughing out loud. But they all nodded in agreement.

"Aw, dang it, all right. You win."

"No," Butterworth told him, "*you* win."

He escorted Festus to an empty barber chair and said, "Close your eyes while I put something pleasant smelling on your face."

"Well, why you wanna do that now? I'll just wash it off in the bath."

"I know, but I wasn't thinking of you, I was thinking of myself."

Festus didn't understand but he did as he was told. *Man, oh man,* he thought, *looking like an important marshal is going to cost me a bundle of money!*

CHAPTER

5

"Well, well, Marshal Haggen," Butterworth exclaimed when Festus emerged from the bath with his face now shaven and his hair short and stylish, "you're not half as ugly as I thought!"

"Thank you." Festus regarded himself in the mirror. "I still think you should have left my mustache."

"No, no! It was too thin. Kind of . . . weedy looking, actually. Marshal Matt Dillon doesn't have a mustache, does he?"

"No, but he ain't short, bent, and bowlegged like me, either."

Butterworth chuckled. "You're not short. *I'm* five foot nine inches and you're a good two inches taller. I'd guess that you are almost six feet tall, and that in your stocking feet."

"Naw."

"It's true!" Butterworth turned to his regular customers, many of whom just came in to sit and socialize each morning for nothing better to do. "Anybody in here know their own exact height?"

"I do," a former newspaperman named Woodson said. "I'm six foot even."

"Then come stand back-to-back with our new marshal. Take off your shoes first, because the marshal is carrying what I suppose were once a pair of work boots."

"Still are boots!" Festus said testily. "And I don't want to—"

"Come on now," Butterworth insisted. "Festus, you said that you were short, bent, and bowlegged. I'll agree to the last two but not the first. Stand up straight."

Festus grumped but everyone seemed so interested in seeing how he measured up against Woodson that he accepted the challenge, sure that he'd measure up much the shorter man.

Buttterworth pushed them together shoulder blade to shoulder blade, with the backs of their heads just barely touching.

"Woodson is a shade taller," one of the onlookers said, squinting hard through his best eye.

"Marshal, stand up straight!" Butterworth ordered, and a moment later he cried, "Aha! Exactly as I thought. When Festus quits stooping, he *is* six feet tall!"

"Really?" Festus asked.

Butterworth motioned his waiting clients over to verify his conclusion. "Agreed?"

They all nodded.

"See!" Butterworth triumphantly proclaimed. "Festus, you are a six-footer!"

Festus shook his head and went over to pull on his old boots. "Hard for me to believe. Next to Matthew, I—"

"Marshal Dillon is a giant," Butterworth interrupted. "Anyone who is constantly around someone that big would just naturally start to feel they are smaller and more insignificant. Marshal Haggen, you are not a short man, and if you made even a little effort to improve your poor posture, you'd greatly improve your self-esteem."

"What's that?"

"It's the way that you regard yourself. If a man *thinks* he is big and strong and *acts* big and strong, then he *is* big and strong."

"Huh?" The man was talking gibberish.

"The mind," Butterworth said, tapping his temple with a manicured forefinger. "We are what we believe ourselves to be. If we feel unworthy, then we *are* unworthy. If we feel successful and proud, then we *are* successful and proud."

"You're losin' me," Festus confessed.

"Of course I am. It's a way of thinking and acting and it is all conscious mind. I, for example, consider myself to be tall and handsome."

The customers laughed, but it was hearty, good-natured laughter, so Butterworth took no offense. "Now, physically, I may not be six feet tall, but that is secondary to the fact that I feel six feet tall and so I am, in my own mind, which is the source of my being."

"Well," Festus said, pulling on his old boots and hitching up his pants. "I don't know about any of that kind of talk, but I am going to buy my new duds right now."

"And a tall, handsome hat," Butterworth advised. "And boots with high heels. And for heaven's sakes, don't buy some plain denim pants and a work shirt! Buy something with color and don't forget a silk bandanna."

"Now, wait a minute."

"And a belt," one of the customers added. "He sure needs a real belt and a fancy silver buckle."

"Yes," Butterworth agreed with a thoughtful frown. "Tell you what, boys, let's *all* go over to York, Hadder and Draper Mercantile and make sure that our friend here is properly outfitted!"

The Centennial's clientele were mostly a bunch of successful retirees and the barber's idea instantly struck

31

them as first-rate. Festus, however, was not nearly as enthusiastic because he knew that agreeing to this plan would cost him far more money than he wanted to spend.

"Ah," he hedged, "you fellas just stay here and relax. No need for you to bother."

"No bother," a retired rancher named E. C. Edwards insisted, "I know high-quality boots and hats and I'll help you pick out the best."

"I don't *want* the best, Mr. Edwards. I don't make that much money and I'd like to keep what I have already saved, if you don't mind."

"Don't worry, Festus, we'll keep an eye on the prices," E. C. promised. "I know Mr. York who runs the place right well, and he'll give you his best price."

The next thing Festus knew, they were all marching down the boardwalk telling everyone they met about how Festus was going to get outfitted. People grinned, some laughed, and a few even fell in with the barbershop contingent, so that they were a crowd when they pushed into Dodge City's largest and most expensive mercantile.

"Mr. York!" E. C. boomed. "As you might have heard, Marshal Dillon broke his leg out in the street."

"I saw it," the proprietor replied, curiously eyeing Festus with his clean-shaven face and short hair. "Awful shame. But what has this to do with —"

"Festus is going to fill in as the marshal of·Dodge City until Dillon is back on his feet," Butterworth announced. "And so he has decided to clean up and improve his image."

"You have?" York asked, looking surprised.

"I guess," Festus answered, "but it was never my intention that everyone in town should make it a grand spectacle. I just want some new clothes."

"And a Stetson, belt, and boots," the rancher added. "We want you to fix Festus up just right."

"And how will you be paying for everything?" York asked, looking skeptical again.

"I got savings in the bank." Festus knew his cheeks were turning red. "Plenty enough to handle what I buy with cash money."

"Very good!" York said with approval. "Let us proceed first to the boots and work ourselves up to the hat. Or would you prefer to go down?"

"Don't matter none to me," Festus said, "but I don't want to buy the best and—"

"Never mind that," Butterworth said. "We told Festus that you would give him a discount, seeing as how he is an underpaid public official and our new interim marshal."

"Sure," York agreed after surveying the expectant crowd, "I used to be a member of the town council and I know what he earns. It isn't very much, that's for certain. Come on, Marshal, let's fix you up fine."

And so they started with the boots. Most men had theirs custom-made, but these days you could buy them in the most common sizes from the factory, and some of these were almost as good as the ones you had made on order. Festus chose a pair that were black and shiny with handsome white stitching. He'd never owned such a beautiful pair and he didn't dare ask their price because he wanted them so bad and everyone thought they were perfect. They even fit.

"You just put them on your feet and put your feet in a water trough for about an hour, then walk 'em dry," old E. C. advised. "That way they'll be a perfect fit."

"I know," Festus said, "I been doin' that for years."

"Now the pants," Butterworth called from over by the clothing section. "He'll need two pairs of pants and at least five new shirts."

"I don't need no five shirts!" Festus screeched. "Mr. Butterworth, you stop that right now or I'll go broke."

"All right, then at least three. But first the pants. Mr. York, nothing baggy like those terrible ones Festus always wears. We need something trim and stylish."

"I have just the perfect pair for him," the store owner

declared with a flourish of his hand. "And wait until you see the fancy new shirts that came in last week! He'll look best in red, black, and green . . . don't you agree, Melvin?"

"Absolutely," Butterworth said. "Bring them on and let's have a good look."

Festus groaned. More and more people were entering the store, too curious to wait until he left. Festus didn't know what to do as women and children, as well as all the folks from the Centennial, crowded around and watched him try on the new duds. Each time he emerged from the fitting room, they clapped their hands or made some loud comment of approval or disapproval.

The entire experience probably took less than an hour, but it seemed to last a lifetime, and it didn't end until he'd bought an ivory-colored Stetson with a fancy rattlesnake-skin hatband and two silk scarves, one red and the other dark blue.

"All right," Butterworth shouted to the townfolk who now packed the store, "we have ourselves a new man! From now on this is Marshal Festus Haggen!"

Everyone broke into applause and Festus drew himself up to his full height in his new boots, grinning like a happy idiot.

"Come over here and take a look at yourself," Butterworth urged.

The crowd parted and Festus waltzed down the aisle to stand before the store's ceiling-to-floor mirror. He nearly fell over with amazement. "Holy hog fat, I don't even look like me," he managed to croak.

"Ah, but it is you!" Butterworth shouted. "It is the *new, confident, successful* you!"

Festus couldn't help turning one way and then the other, regarding himself from all the frontal angles. "Well, I wish my mama could see me now," he said with a happy chuckle. "And I can't wait to see the looks on Matthew, Doc, and Kitty's faces!"

Mr. York tugged on the marshal's new shirtsleeve. "You really should have a suit coat to go with your new outfit. Something that—"

"Oh, no sir," Festus told him, vigorously shaking his head back and forth so the man would know he was real serious. "I'm almost afraid to ask what I already owe."

"Including that fine leather belt that Mr. Edwards insisted upon, it all adds up to just about one-eighty," the store owner told him. "But if you want, I'll throw in a forty-dollar suit coat and extra pants for only twenty more dollars and make it an even two hundred. How about it, Marshal Haggen?"

Festus wanted to say no. Something from way down deep in his hillbilly heart begged to cry out that this whole thing was just a big, dumb mistake. That the attractive and important-looking gentleman in the mirror wasn't Festus Haggen, it was just a fraud.

Yet his shining reflection argued otherwise. It said that he owed it to himself, to Matthew, and to the town of Dodge City to look his very best as town marshal. No one would ever mistake him for famous and strikingly handsome frontier celebrities like Buffalo Bill Cody or Wild Bill Hickok, but now he didn't look so sorry and unimportant anymore.

"All right," he said firmly and quite without conscious thought, "a suit coat and pants and two hundred dollars even!"

The crowd overheard and burst into applause.

CHAPTER

6

D oc arrived that morning just in time to see Festus
and his crowd of admirers exit the big mercantile on
Front Street. He was driving his buggy and looked haggard from lack of sleep and worry.

"Hey, Doc!" Festus called, anxious to show off his new
image. "How are you?"

Doc pulled on the reins and stared at his old friend for
a moment, then wrinkled his nose, scowled, and asked,
"For the love of Pete, what have you done to yourself,
Festus?"

It was not the response that Festus had hoped for or expected and he was taken aback. "Well, Doc, I am
changin' my image. Matthew, he made me the town marshal and I figured I had to clean up and look respectable."

"Hmmph!" Doc snorted. "A bunch of silliness, if you
ask me. How is Matt doing?"

Festus was so hurt that it took him a moment to form
even a simple answer. "Why, he's much better, Doc. Miss
Kitty and me set his leg straight."

"Did you do it right?"

"I hope so." Festus was getting irritated. "Why don't you like my clothes and everything I done to make myself look better?"

"'Cause it ain't the real you," Doc snapped before continuing up the street to the livery.

"Never mind him," E. C. said, probably noting how crestfallen Festus appeared. "Some folks just can't stand to see other folks lookin' better than themselves. And Doc is real tired."

"I guess that's it," Festus said, shaking off his disappointment. "I better go help him and find out if it all went okay with Mrs. Johnson."

"You take my advice," Butterworth offered, "you leave him alone until he gets a drink or two under his belt and then some sleep. Doc can get as touchy as a teased snake."

"No," Festus said, "I better go help."

When he arrived at the livery, Doc was just collecting his medical kit and leaving the rest to the stableman. "Here," Festus offered, "let me carry this for you."

"Festus, you smell like a woman and you're dressed up like a riverboat gambler! Why'd you let them go and gussy you up like this? You look ridiculous."

"No I don't, Doc! I seen myself in that big old mirror over at the mercantile and I look pretty handsome."

"You think so?"

"I . . . well, not as handsome as Matthew or some, but more handsome than I ever looked before," Festus lamely added.

"You'd do well to remember that foolish pride cometh before a fall."

"What do you mean?"

"Festus, I mean that one of your most endearing qualities has always been that you didn't let anyone mess you up and make you try to be what you are not. But that has just changed and I am truly sorry. You were an original and now you've become just a copy of someone's idea of a gentleman. It's a pity when someone loses his own unique originality, and that was the one thing you had plenty of, to my way of thinking."

"But, Doc, Mr. Butterworth says we are what we think we are."

"He what?"

"You know, if you think you are handsome, tall, or strong, then you are."

"Oh, poppycock! If you're a short man, like myself or Butterworth, all the thinking in the world that you are tall isn't going to raise your head one danged inch! It might swell your *hat size,* but it won't make you any taller."

"I was just trying to improve myself," Festus said, feeling deflated. "And you shouldn't ought to try and take that away from me."

"Never mind, you. Let's go see what kind of a job you and Kitty did setting Matt's leg. I sure hope that you did it right, 'cause it's going to be an agony if I have to try and straighten it out again."

"We did the best that we could. I thought you'd be pleased and want us to go ahead. Kitty thought so, too."

"I can't fault you for thinking that."

"You're cranky as a teased snake, Doc. How'd it go with Mrs. Johnson?"

Doc Adams took a deep, deep breath, then expelled it slowly. "The poor woman died in childbirth."

Festus blinked, then said, "I'm sorry."

"Me, too. I expected a few minor complications. That's why I couldn't leave to help Matt. She was small, her husband is very big, and she wouldn't leave her homestead and come into town, where I could have had some help. It was a tragedy, Festus, and I laid her out on the floor because my back gave out and I couldn't lift her into the buggy. You'll need to get Percy Crump to retrieve the body and give the woman a Christian burial."

"I don't expect he will drive out that far."

"Then *you* do it!" Doc snapped. "Stop admiring your-self and do what has to be done for the poor woman."

Festus let Doc walk on over to the Long Branch by himself. He wasn't angry anymore, though. Doc hated to lose a patient and he'd just lost two—Mrs. Johnson and her baby. That was enough to make any man upset.

"I can't leave my business here and take the hearse all the way out to the Johnson homestead," Percy Crump whined. "Festus, I got important stuff to do!"

"Like what?"

"Well, I got to make Mrs. Johnson a casket." Crump avoided Festus's eyes. "Did Doc say if the baby was born or not?"

"No."

"Well, you ought to ask him so I can have a baby's cas-ket ready, if necessary. And did those folks have *any* money?"

The question caused something to snap deep inside Festus. He reached out, grabbed the town's only under-taker by the front of his shirt, and hauled him to his toes. "Dammit, Percy! You go out there and you take care of your business and then you bring that poor woman and her baby—if there is one—back here and we'll find the money to bury them right! Do you understand me!"

"Yes, sir!"

"Now git out of here, and you'll drive all night if you have to, but bring them back by tomorrow and let's bury them right away."

There was raw fear in Crump's eyes. "I . . . I could take a shovel and just bury them on their homestead, Marshal. Maybe that's the way that they'd want it anyhow. I'll bet Mr. Johnson would take comfort in having the graves right on his place so he could be close to them when he returns."

Festus knew that the undertaker's suggestion was born of convenience. Percy Crump didn't want to haul bodies to Dodge or even make them coffins.

"All right," he said, "but you take a coffin out and do the job right. Six feet deep and a cross with their names."

"What about the baby?"

"If there is one, bury it with its mother."

Festus released Crump and started for the door, where he turned and jabbed a finger at a man he had never respected. "And Percy?"

"Yes, Marshal?"

"I'll be passing through there before long and checking on the grave. I might even take a shovel, and gawd help you if she's buried without a coffin."

"Yes, sir! And . . . well, I know you'll help get me the money for repayment, Marshal Haggen. Mr. Dillon would see that things were made right by me."

"Then so will I."

Festus was starting to discover that there were things about being the marshal that he didn't like. For example, this talk about burying poor Mrs. Johnson out on her place was upsetting. In truth, he'd rather have gotten into a fight with a Texas cowboy than consider the possibility of two bodies lying on a homesteader's rough plank floor. But he'd done his job and knew that Matthew would approve.

His next stop was at the bank, where he needed to withdraw the two hundred dollars to pay for his new outfit. Festus marched up to the teller, a nice young man named Willy Wilson. "Willy, how you doin' today?" he said amiably. "I need to draw out some cash."

Willy just stared. Finally, he said, "Yes, sir. But . . ."

"What's wrong?"

"Well, who *are* you?"

"I'm Festus, for cryin' out loud."

"Oh, my gosh! What happened? You look . . . great!"

Festus didn't know whether to hit the teller or to thank him. He did neither, but Willie's expression begged for an explanation, so he said, "Matthew broke his leg in the line of duty and he's asked me to be the new marshal. But your boss, Mr. Brodkin, he's going to recommend to the town council that they find an experienced lawman. Until then, I felt I needed to improve my image."

"Well, you sure as the dickens have! My, oh my! I didn't even recognize you."

"Now that you do, can I have two hundred dollars out of my savings account. I need it to pay for these duds, the boots and—"

"Let me see that hat! Why, you got a real haircut, too!"

While Willy ran his fingers over the soft new felt brim, Festus was aware of the unwelcome attention he was receiving from the other customers and the entire banking staff. He did not like to be the center of attention and would have much preferred to be waited upon like anyone else, without any fuss.

"Wow! I'll bet this set you back at least forty dollars!"

"I'm not sure. Mr. York over at the mercantile says the total bill amounts to two hundred dollars. That's how much I need to withdraw today."

"Here," Willy said, handing him back the beautiful Stetson. "Would you pull up your pants a little and show me those shiny new boots?"

"Oh, I guess." Festus was beginning to feel a bit foolish as he raised his pant leg.

"Boy, those are pretty!" the teller exclaimed, poking his head out of his teller cage and gawking.

"Is something going on here that I ought to know about?" Mr. Brodkin asked, arriving to address his exuberant employee.

"Yes, sir," Willy replied. "Take a look at the new Festus Haggen!"

Brodkin was not impressed with much of anything other than himself, but his altered expression told Festus that even the banker was shocked and amazed at the new Festus Haggen.

"Well, my goodness gracious! What have you gone and done to yourself, Festus!"

"As long as I am temporary marshal, I decided that I ought to look like a credit to Dodge City. So I bought these clothes. Do you like 'em?"

"Very nice. Very nice indeed! And you've done something else."

"I took a bath, got a shave and a haircut."

"Remarkable. I find it hard to believe you are really Festus."

He blushed with embarrassment. "I guess I do look a lot different."

"You seem a lot taller, too," Willy observed. "How high are your new boots' heels? Four inches at least, I'd bet."

"Mr. Butterworth told me to stand straight, and so that's what I've been trying to do this morning. I got measured and they say that I'm a six footer. I never realized that."

"You look like a new and much better man," Brodkin said. "So what can we do to help you today?"

"I need to draw out money from my savings account."

"How much?"

"Two hundred even."

"You have that much saved?" Brodkin asked, again looking amazed.

"I've a lot more than that, sir. You can ask Willy. He's been making my monthly deposits for the last couple years."

"It's true, Mr. Brodkin. Festus has quite a nice account with us now."

"On your pitiful salary, Haggen?"

"I don't spend much," Festus explained. "I live real simple and have no one to support."

The banker's eyes bored into Festus as if he were making a discovery of some importance. "Marshal Haggen, please step into my office while Willy withdraws your cash."

Festus had never been asked into the back offices and certainly not to the office of the bank's president. He

42

tipped his hat, ducked his head in greeting to the others on the staff, and was ushered into Brodkin's office.

"Have a seat, Marshal."

"This is real nice, sir," he said, admiring the velvet curtains, the plush carpet, and the enormous mahogany desk, complete with an impressive matched silver pen-and-paperweight set. "You sure have a fine office. Nothing like the one that Matthew and I use."

"Listen," Brodkin said, sliding in behind his huge desk. "About your replacement."

"Have any luck?"

"No," Brodkin told him. "It's nearly impossible to get a qualified temporary replacement in your dangerous line of work. We sent out a few telegrams, but the only reply we received was from Mr. Waco Black."

"He's awful!" Festus cried. "Waco ain't nothing but an outlaw hisself. He calls himself a bounty hunter, but he's never brought anyone in alive. Matthew has been trying to get some evidence to arrest and send him to prison for years."

"I know that, and so does the council. I've even heard that the man has six notches on his gun. The very last thing we need in Dodge City is a corrupt opportunist and a cold-blooded killer."

Festus had never seen Waco Black, but the mere mention of his name was enough to make his stomach churn with worry. "Is Waco comin'?"

"We immediately sent a telegram declining his offer of employment but . . . well, who knows?"

"That's right, Mr. Brodkin. Waco might still arrive expecting to be hired."

"Then I'm afraid that you will have to inform him otherwise, Marshal Haggen."

Festus wasn't pleased and he came to his feet. "Mr. Brodkin, Waco Black is a very determined man who would do about anything to get his teeth into Dodge City. He might not go away easy."

"I'm sorry. I know that the very last thing you need is to face a seasoned killer, but we had no idea the man would apply."

"I already got enough to worry about without the likes of a man like Waco."

"I sincerely apologize for the town council. I can't imagine how he found out we needed a replacement. Which brings me to another issue."

Festus was steaming.

"I am going to recommend to the town council that *you* be retained as Matt Dillon's replacement."

"You are?"

"Certainly! Look at yourself. You're a new man. One that we can feel good about, instead of ashamed of."

"You was ashamed of me?"

"Well, we were hardly pleased," the banker replied with a casual wave of his hand. "We'd spoken to Dillon on a number of occasions, urging him to make you toe the mark, so to speak. But I guess he never acted upon our suggestions."

"Matthew never said you people were unhappy with the way that I looked. I thought I was doing a pretty good job."

"Oh, you were! But just as you have discovered the importance of your own self-image this morning, so have we discovered that Dodge City needs to improve its image. Times are changing, Marshal Haggen. Dodge will continue to grow and to prosper. In time, well, we might even be looking at becoming the capital of Kansas."

"Is that possible?"

"Of course. And to be successful in that goal, we have to dress up and look as if we deserve the best that Kansas has to offer."

"I see," Festus said, a little overwhelmed by all this talk and especially by Brodkin's change of heart regarding a replacement.

"Marshal, I can only say that I am delighted you have seen the light, so to speak."

"Thanks."

"And how is Dillon, by the way?"

"You haven't visited him?"

"Why should I?"

Festus didn't have an answer for that, but it just seemed like Brodkin might have met with Matthew and discussed the future and his temporary replacement. Apparently, no one on the entire town council had even bothered.

"I had best get my money and go pay off Mr. York."

"Money well spent."

"I am glad that you approve," Festus said, still troubled by this conversation and especially by the possible interference of a noted gunman and backshooter like Waco Black.

"Good day, Marshal. And by the way, I have some other good news."

"Mrs. Johnson and her baby died, so I could use some."

"Who was she?"

Festus started to explain, then just shook his head. "No one you'd know."

"My good news is that the town council has voted to pay his temporary replacement *and* Dillon full wages until he is ready to fully resume his duties. That means that *you* can expect a significant pay increase until Dillon returns, which we expect to be in no more than one month."

"He might take longer," Festus said, heading for the door. "It was a real bad break."

"I'm sure that it was, but Dillon is strong as a horse and he'll perform his duties next month even if he has to do it on crutches."

Festus was tight-lipped as he took his cash from Willy and headed back out onto Front Street. What he needed to do now was to have a long talk with Matthew.

CHAPTER

7

Festus paid off his bill at the mercantile and headed for the Long Branch. It was slow going, though, because everyone wanted to tell him how fine and much better he looked. He kept his shoulders pulled back a little, too, and his chin up the way a man did who had important business to handle.

Best of all, he happened to meet Skinny Sally coming down the boardwalk, and when she finally recognized him, she gaped and whispered, "Festus?"

"It's Marshal Haggen," he replied, even tipping his hat brim the way Matthew did to all women, no matter how low or mean their station.

"My heavens, man, what happened to you?"

"I got me a whole new image."

Sally wagged her head back and forth. "Well," she said, "the billy goat has turned into a peacock! You even smell nice."

"Glad you like it, Miss Sally. How is George Apple feeling these days?"

"How should I know? George up and ran out early this morning. I checked at the livery and his horse was gone. I figure he went racin' after his friends and is already halfway down to Texas."

"He'll probably be back next spring."

"Don't matter to me none," Sally said. "Business is always good when the cowboys arrive. And with the first trail herd into Dodge, there's enough of 'em to go around for all us girls."

"You ever think of going respectable, Miss Sally? You know, takin' a husband and all that?"

Her laughter was harsh. "No."

"Well, you ought to."

"Festus, if you're proposin' marriage to me, I accept."

He felt his cheeks warm and it didn't help that she cackled even louder to see him blushing. "Naw, I ain't the marrying kind. Probably never will find a woman who'd put up with me."

Sally turned serious. "I would have agreed with that when you looked and smelled like a billy goat. But I can see that's changed. Festus, behave yourself, show some manners, and some respectable woman will be trying to lasso and drag you to a preacher."

"Aw, Miss Sally. I'm still Festus Haggen, the hillbilly."

"Yeah, but you've gotten real shiny. Mark my words and be careful, Festus. I'd marry you myself, except you wouldn't be happy with me and you'd get fired."

The talk had gotten uncomfortable, so Festus dipped his chin, touched the rim of his new Stetson, and continued on down to the Long Branch Saloon.

"Well I'll be a ring-tailed raccoon!" Sam the bartender shouted when Festus walked in. "Boys, take a gander at Marshal Festus Haggen!"

They all turned and stared, a few whistling. Festus was glad it was dim because he felt like seven kinds of a fool, and so he hurried on past the grinning monkeys to see Matthew.

"Come on in," Matt called.

"How you—"

"Festus?" Matt gaped. "What . . . what happened to you!"

"I got myself a new image. I couldn't much stand the idea of being my old self and being town marshal, so I shined myself up a bit. Do you like it?"

"Why, I sure do. Come on over here and let's see you up close."

Festus approached the bed.

"Why, you even smell good."

"Matthew, I didn't come here to be admired," Festus said peevishly. "I came to see how you was doin' and how that leg is healin'."

"Doc says that you and Kitty did a first-class job resetting the bone. No one was more relieved to hear that than I was."

"I'm real glad."

"Pull up a chair." Matt grinned. "I can't believe that I'm looking at my deputy."

"I got a haircut, too."

"I noticed. And I never saw your face so plainly before. Festus, you're not as ugly as everyone thought."

"Aw, Matthew, I ain't gonna win any prizes. But I do feel better about myself."

"You should. That outfit must have cost you a small fortune."

"Two hundred for the works."

"It was worth it. I especially like that snakeskin hatband and your fancy boots."

"They ain't near as comfortable as my old pair, but they'll get better soon as I put 'em in a water trough and then wear 'em dry."

"I expect that they will."

"Matthew, I just saw Mr. Brodkin and he says that we're both gonna be paid as marshals for the next month. But he says he'll only pay you after that."

"We'll see," Matt replied. "Doc doesn't believe I'll be able to do much for at least a couple of months and you're going to be paid as a marshal as long as you've got the duties and responsibilities."

"Did you know the town council sent telegrams out, looking for a replacement?"

"Why the devil did they do that? I told 'em that you could handle the office until I got back."

"They didn't like my image. Mr. Brodkin told me so. Don't blame him much. Anyway, guess who answered the call?"

"Charley Gray over in Wichita?"

"No, Waco Black."

Matt's eyes widened. "Are you serious?"

"I am. Mr. Brodkin told me he did. They sent him back a telegram saying they didn't want him for the job, but, well, you know he might come here anyway and try to horn into our office."

"I wouldn't trust that killer as far as I could throw him *and* his horse!"

"I know that," Festus said. "But that don't change the fact that he might come lookin' for your job."

"If he does, I'll climb out of this bed and send him packing. I've been trying to get him nailed with solid evidence of murder for I don't know how many years now. But he's crafty, Festus. He's a hired gun, but he operates on the idea that dead men tell no tales. When Waco Black finishes a job for hire, there are no living witnesses."

"If he shows up in Dodge City, I'll disarm and send him back to wherever he came from in a big hurry."

"No," Matt argued, "if he shows up, let me know and we'll both give him a quick send-off. I may have a busted leg, but I'm not completely helpless. You've got to promise me that you'll do as I say."

"Yes, sir, but—"

"No buts or maybes, Festus! Waco Black isn't a man to be taking chances with and the only thing he respects is force. He knows that I have been trying to collect evidence on him for murder."

"Didn't he once swear to kill you?"

"He did. About eight years ago Waco came to town gunning for a young rancher that someone wanted dead. I got wind of it and laid a trap, but he heard what I was up to and lit out fast. I understand that I cost him a thousand dollars in blood money."

Before Festus could form a comment, Kitty appeared in the doorway. "Why, look what we have here! Festus, you look terrific! I'd heard from everyone that you'd changed your entire appearance, but I never imagined how handsome you were!"

"Aw shucks, Miss Kitty, Matthew is handsome. I ain't."

"I'll bet my girls say different. They're going to be after you like flies on sugar."

"Skinny Sally said she'd marry me but knew I wasn't interested."

"Of course you weren't," Kitty agreed. "You're going to have some young and pretty girls of marriage material after you before long. So don't you mess with anyone like Sally."

"No, ma'am!"

"Doc said we did a fine job. I wish you'd have been here when he examined Matt's leg. We did ourselves proud."

"I am mighty pleased to hear that."

"So," she asked, "how does it feel to be the marshal of Dodge City?"

"It feels good . . . most of the time."

"Kitty," Matt said, "he tells me that Waco Black might be coming to Dodge to try and take my job. That really worries me."

"It should," Kitty answered. "I still remember how cussed mean he was. You be careful, Festus. Don't let him get the drop on you."

"No, ma'am."

They commiserated over the news of Mrs. Johnson for a few minutes and Matthew seemed pleased about the way Festus had ordered the undertaker to go out and give them a proper burial.

"That Percy Crump is the most avaricious man I've ever known," Kitty said.

"Aver . . . what?" Festus asked.

"Greedy! Just pure and plain greedy."

"I couldn't agree with you more," Festus said. "He wouldn't have gone if I hadn't threatened him with bodily harm and promised he'd get some pay."

"Doc feels awful about that," Matt told them. "I've never seen him so downhearted."

The talk went on for several minutes, then Festus figured it was time he got to work. "I'd best go make the rounds and check on the bulletin board outside the office in case anyone needs help. I'll be back soon."

Festus went out to the office and there was a note on the board. It read: I MEAN TO BE THE NEXT MARSHAL OF DODGE CITY. NEXT TIME, LEAVE THE DOOR UNLOCKED SO I CAN TAKE THE OFFICE OVER PRONTO!

Holy cow, Festus thought as he whirled around, hand closing on the butt of his six-gun, *Waco Black is already here!*

CHAPTER

8

Festus was headed back to the Long Branch to ask Matthew how he wanted to handle Waco when a tall, very thin man wearing a black silk vest, pants, and boots stepped into his path.

"You must be Deputy Haggen," the almost cadaverous stranger offered. "I understand you just got all duded up thinkin' you were going to be the new marshal of Dodge City."

"I . . . I *am* marshal. Who are you?"

"Waco Black." The man took a few steps closer. "Where is Matt Dillon?"

"I . . . I don't guess that's any of your concern."

"Oh, I beg to differ with you on that one. I heard he's laid up for a while."

"He'll mend."

"Maybe." Black's eyes dropped a little to the gun on Festus's hip. You any good with that pistol?"

Festus wondered if he was about to become the most

short-lived marshal in history. "I can hit what I aim for, if that is what you mean."

"That's better than a lot of men. Most get all scared and quivery, and they hit everything but what they want to kill. You ever *killed* an armed man, Deputy?"

"I . . . I told you I am the marshal." Festus caught the reflection of himself in the store window to his left. He threw back his shoulders. "And I'll tell you one more thing . . . you ain't going to be Matthew's replacement as marshal of Dodge City."

The man's smile was reptilian. "Who says, Deputy?"

"I do."

"Hmmm. Now, ain't that queer? For you see, I traveled more than two hundred miles for the job. That's a long, long way to ride for nothing."

"A lot of men have ridden farther for less."

Waco stepped a little closer. He was wearing only one pistol on his left hip and it rested high and butt forward, telling Festus the gunfighter favored a cross draw. Waco drew a cigarillo out of his vest pocket, lit it, and smoked for a moment, eyes never leaving Festus. He gave the impression of a rattler about to strike.

He's trying to break my nerve and make me run, Festus told himself. *Waco Black would rather I run than fight.*

That simple realization gave Festus a nugget of hope. It reminded him that any man who went into a gunfight was putting his life on the line, knowing that unexpected things could and often did happen. Being just fast wasn't enough. Even being fast and accurate wasn't always quite enough. Sometimes luck played a part, and no man knew if this was his lucky day or not.

"We got a problem, here, Deputy. I want Dillon's badge, which I can see you are wearing."

Festus's throat was drier than desert dust and it sounded funny when he replied. "And I'm going to keep on wearing it."

"Nobody will admire it pinned to your chest in a coffin," Waco said as smoke trickled out his thin nostrils. "But supposin' I was to let you stay on the job as deputy? I like a man with some backbone . . . so long as he ain't completely stupid and realizes his superiors. But first, where is Matt Dillon?"

"He's probably got you in the sights of his rifle right now," Festus lied.

The lie had an effect. Waco's pale, yellow-flecked eyes moved even if his slender body did not.

Festus cleared his throat. "I want you to leave Dodge City right now."

"You what?" Waco focused on him once again.

"Leave Dodge City. Get on your horse and ride out."

Waco snorted with scorn. "Deputy, are you a family man with a sweet little woman and a couple of kids? If you are, then you need to open that door, turn around, and then run like a jackrabbit."

"I'm not going anywhere, and you ain't getting the key," Festus heard himself say.

"We'll see about that."

Festus shifted his hand closer to the butt of his six-gun and said a little prayer his mama had taught him as a boy. He could feel a trickle of sweat running down his backbone and he guessed he was about to die.

Suddenly a very calm voice said, "Mr. Black, I hope you have enough to pay me for my medical services."

Waco twisted around to see Doc with a double-barreled shotgun aimed straight at his narrow chest.

"Who the hell are you?"

"Dr. Galen Adams, whose services you are just about to badly require."

"Doc, you're an old man and you got no business interfering," Festus protested.

"Well," another voice joined in, "Doc may be old, but I'm not!"

They all looked up on the balcony to see Kitty holding

a Winchester. "And I don't care if you have enough money to pay Doc or not, because, mister, your next stop is going to be the *funeral parlor.*"

Festus seized the moment and drew his gun. "Don't move!"

Waco Black knew when to fold his hand. He inhaled deeply, causing the tip of his cigarillo to turn cherry red, then he smiled that terrible, frightening smile and slowly raised his hands.

"I know when I'm not welcome. I'll be leaving right now."

"And I'll see that you do," Festus told the gunslinger.

Waco's horse was only a half block up Front Street, tied before the Alhambra Saloon. With Doc at his side holding that shotgun and Kitty still keeping the killer in rifle range, Waco Black had no choice but to climb on his weary mount. He looked around to see that most of the merchants were standing in their doorways grim-faced . . . and armed to a man.

"No, sir," Waco said, "this is *not* a friendly railhead town! Why, I wouldn't have wanted to be marshal of a place this downright unfriendly."

He hurled his cigarillo into the dirt and slowly reined his horse away from the hitch rail. Even then Festus was not entirely sure that he would not draw that pistol and try to kill him in the blink of an eye. But Waco Black had other thoughts and other places to go . . . after a last piece of advice.

"The thing about friends, Marshal, is that there is a good part . . . and a bad part. The good part is when they are around to stand beside you. That is a worthy act."

Waco took a deep breath and gazed up and down the street. "But the bad part," he continued, "is when they *aren't* around to back your play. Then it's just you and whatever is about to end your life."

"I'll take my friends and my chances. Now git and don't ever come back to Dodge City."

"Don't expect that I will. Nothin' here worth comin' back to see."

Waco touched his heels to the sweat-soaked flanks of his horse and galloped out of town, heading west toward Colorado.

"Holy cow!" Doc breathed, lowering the shotgun. "Did you look into that man's eyes? I mean, *really* look into them?"

"I did," Festus said, waving up at Kitty to show her how much he appreciated her act of bravery. Kitty waved back and disappeared.

"I never saw eyes like that in a man," Doc said. "They were a medical marvel! He had the eyes of a . . . well, a lizard or a snake."

"He had yellow eyes," Festus said. "At least they looked like they were kinda yellow to me."

"Gold, I thought," Doc ruminated. "If we'd have had to kill him, I swear I'd have removed those eyes, dropped them into a bottle of formaldehyde, and sent them off to my old alma mater for further study."

"Doc, are you pullin' my leg again?"

Unable to keep a straight face, Doc burst out laughing. And despite the absence of anything really funny about what had just transpired, Festus did, too.

Matt wasn't laughing, though. When Festus went up that evening to give him an account of what the gunfighter had said and done, Matt listened in tight-lipped silence. "I'm glad that you handled him, but I'd have liked it even better if you'd arrested the man."

"For what?"

"For posing a threat to public safety and for threatening your life. If you'd have arrested Waco while you had the drop on him, you could have sent telegrams out asking if there was a warrant for his arrest. My guess is that there might have been. In that case, he'd have gone be-

56

fore the judge and we'd finally have gotten him sent to prison."

Festus was more than a little disappointed. "Well, Matthew, I wasn't thinking it all out thataway. Mostly, I was just thinking about how to save my hide and make sure that he didn't get into our office or come up here a-lookin' to settle the score with you."

"I can appreciate that," Matt replied. "But the thing of it is, once you have the drop on a man like Waco Black, you have to make the most of your advantage and try to put him away. Otherwise, he's just going to ride on down the line and bully or ambush someone else . . . and it will probably be another lawman."

"I understand."

"You keep a close eye on your backside, Festus. A man as evil and twisted as Waco Black might take it into his head to return one of these nights with no other purpose in mind than to ambush and kill you. He'd probably aim for your gut so that you would hear his laughter as you lay squirming and dying in the street."

Festus shuddered.

"I'll be careful," he promised.

"I'm proud of you for not backing down, but I'm not a bit surprised. You've shown the people that you not only can *look* the part of a town marshal, but that you can *act* like one. Nice going, Marshal Haggen."

Those words of congratulations erased all the disappointment he'd just been feeling and Festus beamed. "Well," he said, picking up his new hat and setting it down straight on his head. "I am hungry and it's dinnertime. I'll see you in the morning, Matthew."

"Yeah," Matt said with a warm smile. "See you in the morning. Tomorrow, Doc says that I can get up and start to hobble around as long as I don't put any weight on my left leg."

"You think you should take the chance so soon?"

"I was hoping that you might be willing to piggyback me down to the office so I could go over some paperwork."

Festus blinked. He stammered. He gulped and then Matthew started to laugh.

"Dang," Festus grumped as he stomped away, "you folks sure enjoy teasin' me a lot!"

CHAPTER

9

Waco Black had no particular place to go and no particular thing to do. He had not lied when he'd told Marshal Haggen that he'd come a long way to take Matt Dillon's job. He'd heard of Matt Dillon's misfortune and had even gotten his hands on a marshal-wanted telegraph way down in Amarillo and started laughing. Waco hated Dillon, one of the few men who'd actually managed to get the drop on him; not once, but twice. And now, his no-account deputy and friends had managed to do the same.

Waco was seething.

Like a lobo wolf always hungry and on the prowl for weakness and opportunity, he'd come to Dodge City on the scent of blood, figuring that he could kill a bedridden Matt Dillon and settle an old score. At the same time he could forcibly take a marshal's job that would open the doors for all kinds of exploitation. Exploitation and extermination were the games that Waco played best. But now he was on the roam again with no opportunities in sight and not much money in his pants pocket. His horse was worn out and he was in a dangerous mood as the sun dipped toward the western horizon and a little prairie farmhouse suddenly appeared.

"That'll do," Waco muttered as he touched spurs to the flanks of his flagging gelding.

As he drew nearer, Waco saw two men and a black buggy out in the backyard. One of the men was shoveling dirt into what Waco was sure was a grave. The other man, dressed all in black, was sitting in the buggy reading a newspaper.

The homestead itself wasn't much. A small house, a larger barn, and a couple of corrals. There were trees, but they weren't very tall yet and Waco could see a garden already going to weeds. A bony brown milk cow grazed at the end of a long rope and chickens scratched yard dust. It was the kind of hardscrabble place that he saw again and again on the vast prairies from the Dakotas to Texas. Waco knew that these people would feed and put him up for the night in return for a dollar. But he would instead rob these pathetic, long-suffering people, who rarely had more than a lousy twenty dollars. But first and most important, Waco was concerned about why someone had died; he wanted to be sure that it was not of a fever or a sickness.

"Hello!" he called out. "Who died!"

"Woman in birth!" yelled the man digging. "You can ride on in without fear of sickness, mister."

Waco was pleased. He rode up to the pair and dismounted. He dropped his reins, and his horse was so tired it groaned and stood with its head canted downward while Waco stepped up to the grave and peered down at a crude wooden coffin.

"Who died?"

"Mrs. Johnson and her newborn," the gravedigger answered, wiping sweat from his brow. "We was supposed to be finished with this job and in Dodge by tonight, but we ain't gonna get it done. The diggin' has been awful hard."

"The dirt is full of rocks, huh?"

"That's right," the digger said, wagging his head and then drawing a red bandanna out of his back pocket to mop his sweaty face. "I had to use a pike to break the top layer of ground. Been real hard work."

The digger was covered with dirt, and streaks of sweat lined his square face. He covered one nostril and blew the other. He looked worse than Waco's horse and was about the gunslinger's own age, mid-thirties. The undertaker, who was clean and cool in the shade of the buggy's covering, was a few years older. He was wearing a nice diamond ring and a gold pocket watch that Waco figured was worth a fancy price.

"Yeah," the digger was saying as he squared the hole at six feet. "The poor woman would have had a son, if they'd lived."

"Damn hard life out here." Waco looked toward the house but didn't see so much as a dog. "Where is her husband?"

"He ran off to a gold strike in Colorado," the digger said with obvious disgust. "Ain't that what they say, Mr. Crump?"

"That's right. He's a fool and will return busted to find he lost the only things he had of worth."

"Damn shame that she died alone out here," Waco said, wondering if she was pretty and could cook.

"Oh, she wasn't exactly alone."

"No?"

"Well, she was," the digger said, wearily leaning on his shovel, "up until the last. Then Doc Adams arrived, but he couldn't save the pair."

The man in the buggy folded his newspaper and glanced at the setting sun. "Pete, I don't have any intention of spending the night at this gawd-forbidden place.

You finish up and we'll drive back to Dodge even if it takes us until midnight."

"What you're saying is that *I'll* have to drive while you nap," Pete snapped with obvious irritation. "Mr. Crump, I'm all played out. We ought to stay and drive back early tomorrow morning."

"That's out of the question. Finish covering the grave over and we'll stick a wooden cross in the dirt and be done with this sad business."

"Ain't you even gonna paint their names on it? The paint is in the back there, along with a brush and all."

"Some other time . . . maybe," Crump said. "Finish up now and let's get going. Marshal Haggen said he'd come by and check and maybe I'll leave the paint and he can do it his damn self."

"Marshal Haggen is coming out?" Waco asked.

"That's what he said." Crump made a face. "And I told him he had better find a way to get me paid. I looked through the house and all I found was two dollars and twelve cents. Two-twelve! Can you imagine a young woman with child living alone out here with only two-twelve to her name!"

"No," Waco said, "I cannot. She mustn't have had much of a husband."

"He was no homesteader, as you can tell from the look of this place and the fields. He was a dreamer and always looking for the easy money. Never held a job that I know of, and he wouldn't have been much of a father to his son."

"Damn shame," Waco said. "I never had much of a father either."

"Same here," the digger said, grunting each time he loaded the blade of his shovel with the rocky earth and then pitched it onto the coffin. "Dust to dust, they say. Mrs. Johnson sure deserved better. I wished I'd have married her, instead of that fat old sow that I got in town!"

Waco was starting to enjoy himself. "Life sure ain't fair."

"You can say that again."

"What exactly happened to Marshal Dillon?"

Crump answered. "He tried to grab a cow pony that some drunken Texan was bucking out on Front Street. He got his leg broken."

"Too bad!" Waco said, not even attempting to look distressed. "He's a load, ain't he?"

"He's all right," Crump said. "Marshal Dillon can get on your nerves, if you know what I mean. I think he's pretty damned arrogant and bossy sometimes."

"Aw, no he ain't!" Pete argued. "Matt Dillon has never said a cross word to me or my sow. He's fair, but he'll not tolerate any breaking of the rules."

"What about that new fella?"

"Festus Haggen?" The digger paused to catch his breath. "He's just a hill-country fella that has been Matt's deputy for the last few years . . . since Chester left."

"He any good with a gun?"

"I expect that he is. He got the drop on one of those Texans and put a sure enough crease in his head. Festus ain't to be fooled with, and he's the kind you might underestimate and then pay the price for it."

"Just keep working," Crump ordered. "We could be out of here at least before sundown if you'd shovel more and jaw less."

Pete swallowed hard and Waco could see that he was a sensitive man. "I don't think you got any room to complain, Percy. I've done every damn bit of the work since we came. All you was supposed to do was to paint their names and the date on that there cross I made, and you didn't even do that!"

"Have you forgotten that I'm paying you? That I *pay* you three dollars every time I need a grave dug? Maybe you'd like me to find someone else to do the work, huh?"

"I can use the three dollars, but this job is worth at least five."

Waco was already wearying of the pair. He loosened his cinch and then said, "I'm going to stay over tonight. Any food in the house?"

"Some," Crump said. "But you can't just stay here without permission."

"Who is left to give it?"

"Well, I don't know, but you can't just stay."

"Aw, let him stay," Pete said. "We already went through everything in the house and there ain't nothing much worth stealing."

"It would be wrong," Crump insisted. "Mister, you could come on back to Dodge City and get a room."

"I already been to Dodge and I ain't ready to go back . . . yet."

"Well," the undertaker said, "you can't stay here. Maybe the barn."

"Why should I sleep in the barn if there's a bed in the house?"

" 'Cause it was the dead woman's bed and she died on it!"

"Don't bother me none."

Crump climbed out of the buggy. "Listen," he said, coming over to stand in front of Waco. "I've tried to explain how it is and why you can't use that house. It's private property."

"You searched it and took the two dollars twelve cents. You robbed it yourself!"

"Pete!"

"Yeah?"

"I think you had better help me out on this."

"Well, I—"

"Pete! If you want to dig any more graves, you'll help me out!"

Pete took a deep breath. He wasn't quite as tall as Waco, but he was far more powerfully built. With the shovel clenched in his fists, he said, "Mister, why don't you just come on back to Dodge City or agree to sleep in the barn tonight before riding out?"

"No." Waco smiled coldly. "In fact, I am thinking that this grave might be deep and wide enough to cover *three* bodies."

Pete licked his lips and Waco saw his knuckles turn white as he tightened his grip on the shovel. "Pete, don't try it."

"Are you crazy, or something?" Crump asked, fear crawling into his eyes even as he tried to muster some bluster in his voice. "I think you had better just ride on out of here, mister!"

"I think so, too," the digger added through clenched teeth.

"No."

Crump's thin lips pursed and he threw his eyes at Pete, who got the message and lifted his shovel before grating, "Ride out, mister. Ride out now."

Waco shrugged and said, "Okay, if that's how you want it, gravedigger."

Pete relaxed an instant and that's when Waco's hand streaked for the gun on his hip. It came up quicker than a man could think.

Quicker than a big, strong, but exhausted man like Pete could think or act. The gun boomed, its retort half-muffled by the fact that Waco stabbed it into Pete's belly. The digger took a step back, then slowly toppled into the grave. He struck the dirt-covered coffin, then rolled in beside it and the hard, rocky wall he'd shaved with the blade of his shovel. Still alive, he cried out and raised one heavily muscled arm. Waco's second bullet passed between his fingers and struck him in the forehead.

"Holy—"

"Freeze or you're dead!"

Percy Crump had started to turn and leap for the

buggy, where Pete's gun lay on the cushion. But he was slow and Waco's warning turned his bones to mush.

"Don't kill me! Please don't kill me!"

"Why not?" Waco asked. "I liked Pete better'n you and I just killed him."

"I . . . I have money. I have money in the bank. I could—"

"Start digging," Waco ordered.

"Huh?"

"Start digging! I want to see you get all sweaty and dirty."

"But . . . but I'm the mortician!"

"You're about to become a corpse."

Crump grabbed Pete's fallen shovel. Terrified that he might be shot and thrown in the grave with the others, he shoveled like a man, not stopping until he was out of breath and the grave was filled.

"Now paint the woman's name and today's date."

"Mister, please!"

"Do it!" Waco looked at the sun, so big and orange as it settled into the gentle rise of a grassy hill. He paid little attention to the undertaker, not noticing how he spilled paint all over himself while fumbling to do as he'd been told.

"You ain't much of a man, are you?" Waco said. "You like to give orders and play the gentleman, but you aren't much."

Percy was almost sobbing. "Don't kill me, please! You can take the woman's money and I have some, too! You can even take my horse and buggy and I'll walk back to Dodge."

"That would do you good," Waco said. "But it wouldn't do much for me."

"Then we could go to the bank tomorrow and I'll draw out my savings."

"How much would that be?"

"Uh . . . three thousand something."

"Liar!"

"All right, closer to two thousand. But it would be yours!"

"Take off your shoes. They might fit me."

"Yes, sir!"

They didn't fit. But Percy's hat fit and it was pretty nice. Waco knew that the pants and coat were too short, but he ordered the undertaker to remove them anyway.

"Now that diamond ring," he said, hefting the gold watch and chain.

"Aw, it was my father's and—"

"I'll shoot that damn finger off if you don't give it to me!"

Percy gave him the ring.

"Now make a run for it," Waco told the man standing in only his underclothes.

"Will you shoot me down?"

"I don't know. Maybe. But I'll give you the count of ten before I decide."

"Oh, please! I—"

"One. Two . . ."

Percy was long past his prime, but he had long skinny legs and he'd once been fast. And so now, as he raced for his life with skinny legs and arms pumping madly, he began to cry, hearing the killer's voice as he yelled out the dying count.

" . . . eight. Nine. Ten!"

Percy thought his heart was going to explode in his chest when he heard the man's gunfire split the twilight silence. But, miraculously, he did not feel pain nor did he stagger and fall. No, his legs were still moving and he flew across the rock-littered prairie homestead.

More shots, then laughter, then darkness, and finally he collapsed in a low place. With thin chest heaving and heart hammering, Percy gazed up at the moon and knew that he was going to live. He did not know why, but he was going to live and nothing . . . absolutely nothing else mattered.

By then, Waco was removing his saddle and watering his horse. He had it all figured out now, he realized as he unbridled and hobbled the animal. The undertaker should live to reach Dodge City and tell Marshal Haggen of the murder and robbery. Haggen would come and then Haggen would die. After that, Dillon would die as well!

"Interesting how things can turn around for a man real sudden like," Waco said as he entered the house and lit a lantern. He trudged over to the kitchen cupboard and found some beans, corn, and potatoes. No meat and no liquor, though.

"Well," Waco muttered as he eyed the dead woman's bed, "tomorrow I'll just shoot and butcher that milk cow. Then I'll sit back and wait for the fool to come and fill up that grave."

CHAPTER

10

It was about two o'clock in the morning when Percy Crump's strength gave out completely. His feet were bleeding and he was cold and shivering, so he staggered over to the roadside and collapsed. He did not awaken until late the next morning.

"This is like a nightmare that won't end," Percy muttered, wincing with pain as he examined the bruised and cut soles of his poor feet.

But then he remembered how Pete Tyler had been gunned down and how his body had pitched into Mrs. Johnson's grave and decided he was lucky to be alive. No, not lucky. Percy reasoned that the killer had simply misjudged his amazing foot speed and then missed.

I saved my own life, Percy told himself. *And now I must be brave and keep going either until I reach Dodge City or someone comes along. But how humiliating to be almost naked!*

With shrill screams of "ouch!" and "oooww!" Percy forced himself to stand, but it hurt so badly that he could only limp back to the road. Then he sat down and wept. He was still weeping and whimpering an hour later when a traveling kitchenware salesman found and offered him a ride the rest of the way into Dodge City.

"You sure are a pitiful sight," the salesman said, hoisting Percy onto his wagon seat. "I guess you just gave up and probably would have cashed in your chips if I hadn't come along and saved your bacon."

"I was nearly murdered!" Percy cried with indignation. "And my gravedigger was murdered!"

For the next three hours the kitchenware salesman, normally a nonstop talker, barely got in a word. Percy Crump recounted over and over the gruesome details of Pete's murder, always ending by saying how he was saved by his wits, bravery, and speed.

"Yeah," the salesman said, "you got the skinny legs of a runner, but you're a little long in the tooth for that sort of thing."

"I am, but when a brave and resourceful man is called upon to save his life, it is amazing what resources he will find within."

"Too bad you couldn't save Pete's life, too."

"Oh, I tried! Believe me, I took extraordinary risks in a vain attempt to save my devoted employee."

"What, exactly, did you do?" the salesman asked, not recalling that Percy had done anything other than run.

"I *fought* the inhuman killer! I knocked him down and beat him savagely with my fists until he was helpless."

"Then why didn't you shoot him?"

"Because . . ." Percy put his forefingers to his head, the better to concentrate. "Because he had a derringer hidden up his sleeve and I thought it best to run."

"But you said he shot at you with a pistol."

"I . . . " Percy frowned. "It might have been his pistol or that derringer. How should I know? Would you have stuck around to see what weapon he was going to shoot at you next?"

"No, sir," the salesman said, "but I'm getting the facts a little confused."

"Never mind the facts!" Percy was not in a good mood. "Are you sure that you can't make this wagon move a little faster?"

"I'm sure. I got a whole bunch of dishes boxed back in the wagon. They're packed in sawdust and all, but they'll still break if I put my mule to a trot. And the pots and pans start banging together and you just wouldn't believe the noise."

"What about a little whiskey?" Percy glanced down at his poor feet and fresh tears flooded his eyes. "I am in *terrible* pain and I've just lost my best friend."

"Your gravedigger was your best friend?"

"One of my best friends."

"I got whiskey, but I paid good money for it and I ain't going to give it away."

"What kind of a man are you? I just fought off a killer and I'm hurting!"

"I picked you up off the side of the road, didn't I? You got money back in town you can repay me with for a bottle?"

"I don't want a whole bottle."

"I sell it by the bottle, not by the drink. Cost you five . . . no, six dollars. I always add a dollar when someone takes a bottle on credit."

"All right! I'll pay you in town, although it seems indeed stingy of you to charge me so much in this time of great personal suffering."

"You won't be suffering much by the time you've drunk a bottle of my whiskey," the salesman promised with a wink.

"I won't drink the whole bottle."

"Then wash out them cuts in the soles of your feet with some of it," the salesman suggested. "Don't matter to me none how you use it."

"You are not a very charitable man!"

The salesman was already sorry he'd picked up this pitiful passenger who could not stop whining, whimpering, and bragging about himself. And he suspected the undertaker was also a liar and that maybe the whole story had been made up, although something bad must have happened to put the man in such sorry circumstances.

"Six dollars and you sign an IOU right now," the salesman said. "And furthermore, I don't want to hear any more about all that killin' business. We're not far from Dodge City and your talk has about worn me out."

"I do not care much for you," Percy snapped. "However, I will sign the IOU and have a drink because my feet are killing me and my nerves need calming."

The salesman pulled the wagon to a halt. He climbed over the seat and fetched a bottle, which he uncorked and generously sampled.

"Just to make sure that it's my best stuff," he explained, smacking his lips. "Here, sign the IOU and you can have the rest."

Crump signed the paper and took a long, long pull on the whiskey. It burned his throat and then created an inferno in his belly, but he kept drinking. After an hour his feet didn't hurt anymore and he was feeling ever so much better. So much better, in fact, that he did not even notice that he was practically naked when the salesman finally turned the corner onto Front Street.

"Mr. Mortician, where do you want to go?"

"Huh?"

"I said, where should I leave you off so you can get my six dollars?"

"The marshal's office, I suppose. Why are all those people laughing?"

"Might have something to do with the fact that you're naked except for your undershirt and pants," the salesman replied, grinning.

"Oh, my gawd!" Percy cried. "Stop the wagon! Turn it around and take it up to my office!"

"Nope. Street is too crowded and the folks here are havin' too much fun. Gonna be good for my business gettin' so much attention. Here we go, the marshal's office."

Percy tried to make a dignified dismount. But he was drunk and so humiliated that he slipped and landed face-first in the dirt. Blurry, half-familiar faces howled with laughter, and the next thing he knew, Marshal Haggen was dragging him inside his office and slamming him down hard in a desk chair.

"What happened to you, Percy?"

"Oh, Marshal, I have a terrible tale of woe!"

Percy buried his face in his hands and bawled. He would have kept it up for some time if Festus hadn't grabbed him by the shoulder and shaken him until his teeth rattled. "Get a grip on yourself and tell me what went wrong out at the Johnson place! Did Mr. Johnson go crazy, or what?"

"Oh no! Pete and I were attacked by a . . . band of killers! They shot Pete but I managed to fight them off and escape."

Festus blinked. "Now, Percy, settle down and tell me the story from start to finish. Don't leave nothing out."

Percy was drunk. His head was spinning around and around and he couldn't keep it straight exactly how many killers had shot Pete and then tried to shoot him.

"There was four—no, six or seven."

"Percy, you got to sober up and tell me the straight story! How many and what did they look like?"

"Marshal, I don't feel so good! Look at the soles of my poor feet and try to imagine the ordeal I've been through and how I've saved my life."

"You're drunk," Festus said, heading over to the coffeepot and pouring a cup for the shaking, crying undertaker. "You're drunk, but you've seen Pete get murdered and you escaped. Now, how many men were there and why did they open fire?"

"How should I know!"

"Was it right at the Johnson homestead?"

"Yes! He shot Pete and his body landed on the coffin and—"

" 'He'?"

"I mean *they*!"

Festus hurried over to the door and shouted, "Someone bring that salesman in here right now!"

The man was brought inside and Festus introduced himself and then said, "What's your name?"

"Owen James. I found this man beside the road."

"Did you get him drunk?"

"No, sir! He did that all by himself."

"Did he tell you what happened to him and his friend?"

"He did."

"Then you tell me," Festus ordered, directing Owen James into Matt's chair and then hovering over him like a hawk. The salesman told quite a different tale, but Festus was sure that it was, at long last, the truth.

"Did he give you a description of the killer?"

"Yes. He said he was tall and thin, wearing a black vest and outfit."

"What about his horse?"

"He didn't say."

"Was it a bay gelding?"

"I don't know. Ask your friend the undertaker."

"I will," Festus said. "But I may need to talk to you again."

"I'll be around selling my kitchen wares, Marshal. I've nothing to hide."

"I know that."

Two hours and four or five cups of coffee later, Festus was certain that Waco Black was the murderer and that he was alone. The description of the gunfighter and his horse left little doubt of the fact. He got Percy home and then was on his way to the Long Branch Saloon to talk to Matthew when Pete's wife came running across the street.

"Marshal Haggen, where is Pete?"

"I'm afraid that he was shot to death," Festus said, removing his hat. "I'm sorry, ma'am."

"Oh no!" the heavyset woman screeched. "Not my poor darling Pete!"

"I'm afraid so, Mrs. Tyler."

Festus knew that the couple had fought constantly and even separated a time or two. It hadn't been much of a marriage, but you sure couldn't tell that now by how the woman was carrying on.

"Are you going to get my Pete's killer? Are you going to do anything at all, Marshal?"

"You bet I will," Festus replied.

"Then do it!"

"As soon as I can."

"What are you waiting for?" the woman yelled, face turning red with anger. "Matt Dillon would be on his horse and going after that killer by now. And here you are doing nothing! What kind of a marshal are you, anyway!"

Festus placed his hat back on his head and tried to excuse himself, but the woman was big and now she was getting angry. Her meaty fists were balled and Festus wondered if she was going to take a swing at him. He sure hoped not, because fighting a woman was against his code, and yet this one would be like fighting a large and furious man.

Kitty saved him. "Mrs. Tyler," she said, rushing over and placing herself between them, "I know that Marshal Haggen is going to arrest your husband's killer. But first, he needs to get all the facts."

Festus didn't hear the rest. He hurried on up to Kitty's room, where he found Matthew sitting up in the bed, looking rested but anxious.

"Festus, I understand that Pete Tyler was murdered and that Percy Crump arrived drunk and in pretty rough shape."

"He'll survive."

"Pull up a chair and tell me what you've found out."

Festus told Matthew as much as he knew, explaining how he'd got most of the straight story from the kitchen-ware salesman. "Matthew, I'm darned sure that it was Waco Black who killed Pete and nearly killed Percy."

"It sounds like something he would do. There is only one real puzzle of a question that concerns me."

"What's that?"

"Why did he allow Percy to escape?"

Festus frowned. "I don't know. I guess it was around dark when the man showed up at the grave. Percy, he can probably still run a little with them long, skinny legs, and he must have just got away in the dark."

"Huh-uh," Matt said, shaking his head. "Waco wouldn't have missed. And if he had, he'd have just climbed onto his horse, run Percy down, and finished him off in the fields."

"I guess you're right, Matthew! Then why?"

"There's only one reason that I can think of."

"Well, sir, I'm a-listenin'."

"He wants you to come out to the homestead so that he can ambush you," Matthew told his former deputy. "He is waiting for you to ride over and investigate."

"You think so?"

"I sure do."

"Then . . ."

"We'll do as he wants," Matt said.

"What is this 'we' stuff?"

"I can ride out with you in a carriage. We'll surprise Waco and then I'll finally have him right where I want him . . . tried for cold-blooded murder, convicted, and then sent to the gallows."

"Now, Matthew, Doc won't want you to—"

"Festus, get a buggy and come around to the back of Kitty's place. I'll be ready in an hour. And bring along two Winchesters and plenty of ammunition."

"Anything else?"

"Yeah," Matt said, "don't tell anyone our plan, especially not Doc or Kitty."

"Matthew, I could sneak up on Waco by myself and—"

"Don't argue with me, and let's not waste any more time talking," Matt ordered.

"Yes, sir."

Festus headed for the door, more relieved that Matthew was coming than he cared to admit.

CHAPTER

11

M att was leaning on a pair of crutches when Festus pulled the buggy around behind the Long Branch Saloon. He was fully dressed and wearing his six-gun.

"Festus, did you bring the rifles?"

"Sure did."

"Good."

"Can I help you—"

"Nope, I'll do fine."

Matt made his slow way over to the buggy, then tossed the crutches in and climbed up beside Festus. "Let's stay on the alley until we're out of Dodge."

"Yes, sir."

Ten minutes later they had cleared the town and were moving at a good clip down the road toward the Johnson homestead. Matt said, "It's good to be out in the fresh air again. I can't abide staying bedridden for long."

"How is the leg mending?"

"Pretty well. You know how Doc always paints the

grimmest possible picture. If I listened to him, I'd be laid up for six months."

"He and Kitty are sure going to have a fit when they learn that you left town."

"I know."

"Are you sure that Waco will still be at the Johnson place?" Festus asked.

"I'm not certain of it, but that is my guess. You see, he hates me with more than his usual passion and I expect he also hates you for getting the drop on him in town and then running him off."

"I had help."

"Yeah, but you know how Waco thinks. Everything is about revenge or getting even. He thrives on feeling insulted and then having his revenge. Money is secondary to evening the score or an insult."

"So how are we gonna do this, Matthew?"

"I don't know yet, but I'd like to capture him alive."

"Well, I sure hope you figure it out before we get there."

"I will," Matt said, taking a deep breath and admiring the way the sunshine touched the browning prairie grass. Now and then he also looked over at Festus, still not able to believe the physical changes that had taken place in his once scruffy deputy. "Festus, how do you like being marshal?"

"Oh, I like it fine. And I'm going to like havin' the extra money, if that comes to pass."

"It will."

Festus drove on a little farther. "But there are a few things that I *don't* much enjoy."

"I'll bet one of them is the politics."

"That's right."

"What else?"

"When I was just a deputy, I left the office behind and gave it no thought until the next day. Now I sorta feel like I'm on duty all the time."

"You are," Matt replied. "As marshal, you have to be ready for anything at any time. If a gunman like Waco Black arrives, you need to be there to greet and explain the rules to him."

"And to back 'em up."

"That's right."

"I do like how people talk to me now." Festus thought about it for a moment, then added, "They don't talk down to me anymore. It's like . . . well, I'm more their equal now that I'm the one in charge."

"I understand that. We all need to feel important."

"Being a marshal makes you feel real important."

Matt thought for several moments, then said, "If you want to be a marshal, maybe you'll be needing my reference when I'm back on the job. I'd be happy to recommend you for any openings that come up, and they do plenty."

"Thanks, but no thanks, Matthew. When it's time to step down and become a deputy again, I'll be ready."

"Maybe, and maybe not."

"What does that mean?"

"It means that once you get used to being the boss and having the authority to make important decisions, it's very hard to give it up, Festus. Now, I'm not saying you won't, I'm just saying that I want you to remember my offer in case you decide you want to go on being a marshal."

"I'll keep it in mind."

"Do that."

They rode in silence for the next few hours; Matt finally broke it when he said, "As I recall, the Johnson homestead sits right out on the open prairie. There's really no hills or trees or anything to give us cover, is there?"

"No, sir."

"Hmm," Matt said. "That's going to make getting in close to Waco difficult. Maybe we should wait and move in on him tonight."

"Maybe."

Matt glanced up at the sun. "It's well past noon. We could hole up beside the river and wait out the daylight."

"Suits me fine."

"All right, then," Matt decided. "That's what we'll do. I'd guess the homestead is another six or seven miles. We'll go in after dark."

"I could use an afternoon nap," Festus said. "I haven't had one since I took your badge."

"Too bad," Matt said without much sympathy.

They pulled into a stand of cottonwood trees and unhitched the buggy, tethered the horse, and napped until sundown, then they sat and talked about nothing particularly important until Matt said, "I think that we should circle the homestead and come in from the west, where he won't be expecting us."

"Then what?"

"You can circle around to the north side and move in on the house. It'll be dark and I'll yell out that I'm just passing through and looking for a place to rest for the night."

"What if Waco opens fire?"

"He won't," Matt said.

"Then what?"

"I'll drive this buggy up into the yard, and when Waco comes out to talk, you slip in behind and get the drop on him."

"It sounds good to me, except that I don't see how you can be so sure he won't just try to shoot you the minute he hears you call."

"I'll try to disguise my voice," Matt said. "And he won't be expecting me because of the broken leg. Just one more thing."

"Yeah?"

"If he even acts like he's going to go for his gun, shoot him in the back."

"Yes, sir!"

"All right, then," Matt said, pushing himself to his foot and then hopping over to his crutches that were leaning against a tree, "let's get this over with."

It seemed to take an awfully long time before they saw the homestead; it would have been easy to miss if the lights weren't shining through the windows.

"Okay," Matt said, reaching for the lines as Festus climbed down. "You take the rifle and circle around to the north, then come in. I'll give you an hour."

"I don't need that long."

"Just to make sure," Matt said. "We have all evening and I don't want you feeling rushed. You have a watch you can see in the moonlight?"

"No, sir."

Matt frowned. "Never mind. You'll be able to see the outline of this buggy and hear me when I call out to the house."

"I sure hope this works."

"It will. You'll have the drop on Waco, and he's not a big enough fool to throw his life away going against us both."

"Is he as good with a gun as everyone says?"

"Yes, he is," Matt replied. "Now go on. Mrs. Johnson didn't leave a dog behind that might see you and start barking, did she?"

"No, sir."

"Good."

Matt watched as Festus lit out across the fields. There was a three-quarter moon and the light was fairly strong, but not so that anyone could see a dark figure moving fast against the backdrop of the gently rolling hills.

The next hour passed slowly with Matt often checking his watch. When the time was up, he laid the Winchester out on the seat where it would be easy to grab and then he unholstered his sidearm and placed it beside his right hip. He was, near as he could tell, ready.

"Hello the house!" he called in a voice that he forced

to a slightly higher pitch when the buggy reached the edge of the yard. "Anyone home?"

Waco's voice called out from inside. "Who are you?"

"Just passin' through on my way to Dodge City. How far?"

"Long ways."

"You mind if I put up my horse and sleep in the barn for the night? I'll pay you."

There was a pause, then: "Sure, go ahead. I'll be waitin'."

"Thanks."

Matt drove forward and then he saw Waco coming out to meet him. The man said, "Barn is over there."

"Oh, sorry."

Matt's hand found his six-gun and he pulled the buggy to a standstill, bringing the pistol up and aiming at the silhouetted figure.

"Waco, you're under arrest. Hands up!"

The gunfighter threw himself sideways as Matt's bullet pierced the empty air. Waco rolled twice and came up firing. His first slug clipped Matt's sleeve and his second was so close behind that the retorts merged. Matt felt a sting along his neck and he returned fire, seeing the muzzle flash of Festus's gun winking in the darkness.

It was over in a heartbeat. Waco was down and Festus was still standing.

"Matthew, don't shoot no more!"

"Is he dead?"

"I'm not sure. Hold your fire."

Matt removed his bandanna and pressed it to the side of his neck. He knew that he was darn lucky only to be scratched. Although aware of his reputation, Waco had still surprised him with the speed of his reaction.

"He's dead, Matthew!"

Matt climbed down from the buggy, then reached for his crutches and managed to get over to the body. "Can you drag him inside?"

"Yes, sir."

When they were inside the house, Matt stared at the body. "How many times did you fire?"

"Twice."

"Well," Matt said, "it's plain from the looks of those wounds that you hit him both times. Nice shooting."

"Thank you. I was closer than you."

"I know, but I still should have hit him. He clipped me alongside the neck."

Festus hadn't noticed the wound until now and he tore out his own bandanna and offered it to Matt.

"Thanks. It will stop bleeding pretty soon."

"Why don't you sit down at the table and let me take a look."

Matt struggled over to the table while Festus followed on his heels, then inspected the wound. "Matthew, you come awful close to getting dead."

"Thanks to you I'm going to be fine."

"Doc is probably goin' to want to put a couple of stitches in this and he's gonna be awful mad!"

"It was worth the risk," Matt answered. "Waco Black has killed a lot of good, law-abiding people."

"He sure was fast."

"Yes, he was."

"I'll find a bandage and we'll do what we can with that wound," Festus said. "And then I'll see if I can find something for us to eat. Waco had his supper already but the stove is still hot."

Matt said that was a good idea. He sat at the table and studied the dead outlaw and gunslinger. "Yes, sir," he said after a while, "I'm plenty happy to have finally put Waco Black away for keeps."

The next morning, Festus loaded Waco and Pete's bodies into the backseat of the buggy and finished covering Mrs. Johnson's coffin.

"This place has got a bloody history now, Matthew."

"Yes, it does."

"I sure am glad that we didn't die here along with them three."

"Four," Matt corrected. "Mrs. Johnson had a son, remember?"

"Oh, yeah." Festus climbed up into the buggy and took the reins. He managed a polite smile and then he turned the buggy around and headed it for Dodge City.

Their arrival caused quite a stir. First, because of Matthew being up and in the wagon, then because of the two bodies resting side by side in the backseat.

"Go find Percy Crump and tell him he's got some unfinished business."

"Percy has taken to his bed," someone said.

"Get him *out* of bed!" Matt ordered.

"Hey!"

"Uh-oh," Festus said. "Here comes big trouble."

They saw both Doc and Kitty marching toward them and Matt took a deep breath. "This was my idea, so you let me take the blame."

"I was a-figurin' to do just that!"

Doc was especially angry. "Matt, if you're going to disobey my orders, what good is having a doctor! And Festus, don't you know that even a little weight on his leg could cripple Matt for life!"

"I'm sorry."

"Well, you ought to be!"

Kitty reached up and touched Matt's leg. "You're wounded."

"It's just a scratch," he told her. "But it probably would have been a lot worse if Festus hadn't been more accurate than I was out there at the homestead."

The people surrounding the buggy heard Matt's words, and suddenly everyone was slapping Festus on the back and congratulating him for killing such a notorious gunfighter.

"Marshal, why don't you just go along and get some

rest," Matt suggested as Kitty helped him down and then gave him his crutches.

"Oh, I reckon I'll make sure that Percy gets out of bed and takes care of these bodies. Especially Pete's. Poor fella deserves a good burial."

"Yes, he does," Matt said as he slowly headed back toward the Long Branch Saloon.

"Did Festus really save your life?" Kitty asked.

"He did." Matt sighed. "When the bullets started flying, it was Festus who shot the straightest."

"Well," Kitty said, "I'm just glad that you are both alive and well and that Waco is dead."

Just before entering the Long Branch, Matt turned and stared up the street to see a crowd following Festus over to the funeral parlor.

"What?" Kitty asked.

"Oh," Matt replied, "I was just thinking how much he has changed . . . both in his own eyes and that of the townspeople."

"He's a completely different man than he was a month ago," Kitty agreed. "But are you sure that it is for the best?"

Matt looked down at her. "What do you mean?"

"I'm not sure that I mean anything," Kitty replied. "It's just that I sort of miss the old grubby but folksy Festus, that's all."

"Yeah," Matt said, "but I think I like the new Festus even better."

CHAPTER

12

"Well, Matt, let's have a look at your neck wound and that leg I ordered you to stay completely off of," Doc Adams groused the moment Matt and Kitty entered the room. "For the life of me, I don't know why people want a doctor when they do whatever they darned well please anyway!"

"Now, Doc, I didn't have much choice but to go with Festus."

"Sure you did!"

"If I'd stayed here, he would have been going alone against one of the most dangerous gunmen I've run up against in years. I'd never have forgiven myself if he'd been killed."

"I expect that is true, but if you caused that mending legbone to shift . . . even a little, you're going to pay for the rest of your life with pain."

"I used the crutches, Doc."

"Is that right?" Doc removed the bandage on Matt's neck and said, "Take a look at this, Kitty."

Her eyes widened with concern. "Matt, this is a lot more than just a scratch."

"I expect it is, but I'll live."

"Well," Doc decided, "another quarter of an inch to the left and the bullet would have nicked the carotid artery and you'd have bled to death for certain."

"I'll admit that I got lucky." Matt shook his head, remembering. "I've never seen anyone that had the reflexes of Waco Black. He was uncommonly quick."

"I should stitch this wound up, but I'm skittish about putting needles in a man's neck," Doc said, more to himself than to Matt.

"Then leave it."

"I will, but you may have a bit of a scar."

"Doesn't bother me," Matt assured him.

"I'll clean the wound and bandage it properly. To be honest, though, it's your leg that really concerns me."

"It'll be fine. I hardly put any weight on it."

"I'll be the judge of how 'fine' it will be," Doc snapped. "Let's take a look before I go any further."

Matt pulled up his pant leg and knew immediately from Doc's expression that he was unhappy. "Hmmph!"

"What's wrong?"

"What's wrong?" Doc rolled his eyes. "In the first place, it's swollen up like you've just been bit by a rattlesnake. And in the second place, it's discolored again. Doggone it, Matt, I sure wish you'd have stayed in bed!"

"Not me. I did what I had to do and it worked out for the best."

"Time will tell," Kitty added. "Look, I've got to get back to work. Doc, do you need anything before I go?"

"Nope."

Kitty left the room and Doc set to work cleaning and then bandaging the bullet crease across the side of Matt's neck. When he was finished, he asked, "Festus killed that Waco fella?"

"Yep."

"What do you make of him?"

"Not much, Doc. Waco is dead."

"I meant the 'new Marshal Festus.' "

"Oh." Matt studied Doc's face, trying to read his thoughts and concerns. "Well, I think Festus is coming into his own."

" 'His own'?"

"Sure! He's taken charge."

"And he might want to *stay* in charge."

"Is that what is bothering you?"

"Yeah, mostly. That, and your broken leg and my rheumatism and all my other aches and pains."

"Festus will be fine. We talked about this very thing on our way out to the Johnson place yesterday."

"And?"

"And Festus told me that he won't mind going back to being my deputy."

"You believe that?"

"Sure, why not?"

"Well, it would take a pretty unusual man to accept a big demotion and not feel a little cheated."

"I told Festus that I'd give him a good recommendation if he wanted to look for a marshal's job. But he said he was happy in Dodge City."

"I don't believe it."

"Why not?"

"Festus has really changed, Matt. Can't you see that the change is a lot more fundamental than just the clothes he's wearing and the fact that he's taking regular baths, shaving, and getting his hair cut?"

"Of course. But—"

"There are new specialties in medicine that deal with the human psyche. Psychiatry is one I feel is most interesting. It deals with physical problems of the brain, but also with why people act the way they do . . . which is psychological. I have been reading a little about the field, and if I were just starting out in medicine, I believe I'd specialize in psychiatry."

"Is that right?"

"Sure. After all these years out on the frontier, I'm convinced that most men and women are sicker in mind than in body . . . yourself included."

"Doc!"

Adams managed a grin. "Only kidding, Matt. But I am serious about the complexity of the mind and of human behavior. And I am going to watch Festus very closely to see how this unravels. Furthermore, I'm going to warn you that despite his assurances that he will be happy to return to deputy status, he might find that impossible."

"Don't you think that you're making this more complicated than necessary?"

"I hope so. I really hope so. Festus is unique and I liked him just the way that he was. I'm not sure that I enjoy the 'new Festus' nearly as much."

"Perhaps that's because he isn't around so often to be teased."

"Maybe," Doc admitted. "Getting back to the point, I'd be willing to bet you five dollars that Festus isn't going to be satisfied being your deputy anymore."

"I'll take that bet," Matt said, extending his hand.

They shook and then Doc asked, "Is Festus really capable of being a town marshal?"

"I—"

"Think it through, Matt. I don't mean is he brave or smart enough, because we both know that he is. I don't even mean is he honest and good enough to be a marshal, because we also know that to be true."

"Then what—"

"I mean is he too naive."

"Huh?"

"You heard me," Doc said. "Is he too blamed *trusting*? We both know that he can't spell the word 'suspicious.'

90

Festus thinks everyone is pure of heart and the bad ones can all be redeemed, given the chance. You and I know far better. Festus doesn't believe that evil really does exist in some men. That could get a marshal killed."

"I see what you mean."

Matt sighed deeply, then closed his eyes as Doc began to bandage his neck. "You're not only worried that we'll lose him, but that he'll be killed because of his trusting nature."

"Exactly!"

Matt kept both his eyes and his mouth closed until Doc finished bandaging the bullet wound.

"Well," Doc asked when finished, "what do you think, or have you just enjoyed a short nap?"

"I admit that I didn't consider the fears that you've just mentioned," Matt replied. "And I also admit that you've just given me more cause to worry, because Festus always does give a man the benefit of the doubt. That, as we both know, could be fatal."

"You bet it could!" Doc squinted and pointed a forefinger at Matt's face. "If you had always used that approach here in Dodge City, you'd have been killed long, long ago."

"So what do you think should be done?"

"Well," Doc answered, "if Festus ever does come to you and confesses that he can't accept being a lowly deputy again and wants to move up, then you're going to have to give him a tough talk."

"About the evil nature of men?"

"And how there are plenty that will shoot a marshal quicker than the blink of an eye. Those same evil men will gut-shoot another human being for no other reason than meanness and their twisted natures."

"All right, I'll do that. But remember that he just killed Waco Black."

"With you standing in front of the man and Festus standing behind."

"I was sitting, Doc. Sitting in the buggy."

"No matter. Sitting or standing, you were in front of the killer and Festus was sneaking up on Waco's backside."

"All right," Matt said, "you've made your point and I'll have a long talk with Festus should he ever decide to quit and look to become a marshal somewhere else."

"That's what I was hoping you'd say." Doc twisted Matt's ankle just a little.

"Ouch!"

"That didn't hurt the last time I tried it. Matt, I'm telling you to stay off this leg."

"I have been, except for this one time."

"No you haven't. Kitty says that you've been coming down to sit in the saloon most afternoons."

"Doc, I'll go crazy up here by myself. And I do have those crutches."

"You're as stubborn as a Missouri mule."

"And you're not?"

Doc started to reply, then snapped his mouth shut and then his medical bag. "I'll go see to it that Percy Crump is taking care of business. His feet are in pretty bad shape, you know."

"I expect so," Matt said. "That would be a long way to walk barefooted. I'll bet he's making plenty of noise."

"He is," Doc replied. "Percy is trying to make himself out to be a big hero. Anybody who knows him knows better. And with you and Festus killing Waco, well, it has taken some of the wind out of Percy's sails. But I do need to watch his feet and make sure that they don't get infected."

"And that he buries Waco and Pete," Matt said. "Especially Pete. How's his widow holding up?"

"She's milking it for as much sympathy as Percy." Doc scowled. "That woman fought with Pete every day of their married life, but now she's trying to convince folks that he was the second coming of you know who and they had the happiest marriage on earth. Some people!"

"Thanks, Doc."

"Save your thanks and pay your bill on time," Doc answered, going out the door.

When he arrived at the undertaker's, he found Festus arguing with Percy over how Pete was going to be buried.

"Doc, he wants to *charge* Pete's widow, for cripes sakes!" Festus exclaimed. "And what with Pete dying after trying to save his life."

"He didn't 'try to save my life,' " Percy said. "I saved my *own* life."

"Pete was working for you when he died," Festus persisted. "The very least you could do is bury him free."

"Why!"

Festus groaned. "Doc, would you talk to this man? Pete's widow ain't got the money for a proper funeral."

Doc was not a man to beat around the bush. "Percy Crump," he said, leveling a finger in the man's face, "you are going to have one very large medical bill on top of what you've already owed me for months. Now, if you'll give Pete a decent burial and quit whining, I'll cut that bill in half!"

"You will?"

"Yep." Doc made a face. "I'll cut it from forty dollars to twenty, but you've got to pay up now."

"Doc!"

"Now, or you owe me the forty. Which is it going to be?"

"Dagnabbit, Doc! You . . ."

"No more whining or I'll put something on the soles of your feet that will really raise your hair and give you cause to scream."

Percy found the twenty dollars and promised to bury Pete free of charge before Doc would tend to his feet. He wasn't happy, but Festus was pleased.

"Thanks, Doc. That is the stingiest man in Dodge City!"

"No," Doc answered, "*you* are."

"Doc!"

"Okay, you were the stingiest. You got any coffee brewing over at the jail?"

"Afraid not," Festus replied. "Besides, I'm due for a shave and my bath."

"Well, well," Doc said, shaking his head, "if wonders don't never cease."

Festus had his bath and shave. He was dusted and powdered and heading out the door when Melvin Butterworth called, "By the way, Marshal, you've become quite the hero in Dodge City! You keep up the good work and Dillon is going to have a hard time getting his job back."

"Oh, no! I aim to become a deputy again just as soon as Matthew is ready to come back to work."

"Be a waste of talent," Butterworth lamented. "But that's your decision to make, not mine."

"Here comes the Texas stage," Festus said. "I like to meet and greet whoever is on it and make sure they don't run afoul of the rules here in Dodge City."

Festus watched the stagecoach roll in and he stood back and waited, feeling important as people passed and greeted or congratulated him. There were a couple of drunks across the street sitting in rocking chairs and pulling on a bottle they'd bought in one of the town's many saloons, but they didn't seem to be too rowdy or bothering anyone, so Festus let them alone.

A few minutes later he was glad that he did remain in place because a beautiful young woman with reddish-blond hair emerged from inside the coach. She said something to the driver that Festus could not hear, then accepted a valise and turned around to survey the buildings up and down Front Street.

Festus was so taken by her appearance that he failed to notice one of the drunks get up and come swaggering out to greet the woman. He swept off his hat and grinned stupidly, then bowed and nearly lost his balance and fell. He would have fallen if he hadn't thrown a hand out and grabbed the woman, tearing down the front of her dress.

For a moment the woman just stared at him in shock, then she slapped the drunk, knocking him down. The man cursed, jumped up, and balled his fists.

"Hey!" Festus shouted, leaping into the street. "Don't you hit that there woman!"

The drunk wheeled around and cursed in the vilest manner. Festus tried to grab the man and shut his filthy mouth, but the drunk tore a knife from out of the top of his boot and lunged forward. The blade ripped through Festus's new suit coat and vest and tangled in his cartridge belt.

"Dammit!" the man yelled. "I'll gut you like a buck!"

"Like hell you will," Festus said, twisting the man's fingers back until one of them cracked and the knife tumbled into the dirt. He hit the drunk twice in the belly and finished him off with a right cross to the jaw.

"Ma'am," Festus said, bowing slightly to the beautiful woman, "I sure am sorry for the greeting you've just received. My name is Marshal Festus Haggen and you have my sincerest apologies."

"Marshal Haggen, are you all right?"

"Yes, ma'am."

"But you've been cut!"

"No, ma'am, just my coat and vest. Don't worry about them."

"I am so sorry this had to happen," the woman said. "I'm Miss Clara Austin from Austin, Texas. And I can't thank you enough for being so brave just now."

Festus reached down and grabbed the drunk by the collar. "It's my job, miss. And, if you'll excuse me, I'll take this jasper and put him in jail."

"You are very kind."

Festus could feel his cheeks burning. "I . . . well, I hope you'll be staying in Dodge for at least a few days."

"I will be."

"Then I reckon I might have the pleasure of seeing you again before you leave."

"I hope so."

"You . . . you do?"

Her eyelashes fluttered and his heart did, too. "Why, of course! And I'd like to fix that coat and vest, if I may."

"Miss, that won't be necessary. We've got a seamstress in town and she can do it just as easy as you please."

"Well, if you're sure, Marshal Haggen."

"I am, miss. Good day to you, now."

Festus hoisted the unconscious drunk up over his shoulder and started off to the jail.

"What a brave and handsome marshal you have here in Dodge," he overheard Clara say.

After that, Festus just sort of floated off to the jail, even with the heavy load he was toting.

CHAPTER
13

That same afternoon, Festus hovered nervously over the town's only seamstress until she could no longer abide his impatience. "Honestly, Marshal Haggen, I don't understand what is the big hurry! You act as if you need this suit right now, either to get married or be buried!"

"Well, ma'am, you see it's my only vest and coat."

"You could still do without for a couple of days and no one would care much one way or the other."

"No, ma'am, all the folks in Dodge City have sorta gotten used to me lookin' nice and I'd hate to change their thinking."

"Marshal, surely you know it is always the *man,* not the clothes, that are important."

"Sure, but—"

"Why, some of the finest gentlemen I've ever known have been the poorest and most God-fearing. They didn't dress well at all, but their souls were clothed in righteousness and piety."

"I expect they were, but—"

"On the *other* hand, Marshal Haggen—"

"Festus. I prefer you just call me plain old Festus like before, 'cause when Matthew comes back, that's what I'll be again."

"On the other hand," she said, totally ignoring his request, "some of the finest-dressed men are the biggest rats in the world. I'm even talking about United States presidents! Politicians clothe themselves well but there are very few of them that have even a thimbleful of virtue! Not a thimbleful!"

"Yes, ma'am."

"So you don't get all fluffed up with yourself and these nice clothes. Hear me?"

"Yes, ma'am!"

"Because clothes do not make the man . . . or the woman." She frowned. "How did this happen, by the way?"

"Well, there was this here fella that was real drunk and he got to actin' ungentlemanly toward this young woman who just stepped off the stage from Austin—"

"Austin, Texas?"

"Yes, ma'am, and—"

"Stephen Austin was a true gentleman, but Sam Houston was not. Still, he was a great man . . . I suppose."

"Yes, ma'am, and maybe Miss Austin is related to Mr. Stephen Austin, but—"

The seamstress's eyes widened. "Do tell? Her last name is Austin and she is *from* Austin?"

"That's right and—"

"Now, *that* is very interesting. You see, I once lived in Austin and I *knew* a few Austins."

"Well, how about that!"

"Yes, it was fascinating. Marshal Haggen, what does this woman look like?"

"Kinda tall with reddish hair and—"

"Then I very much doubt she's a true Austin, because they had darker complexions and I don't remember any of them having red hair. But some of them were quite tall."

"Her eyes are green."

"Hmm, maybe she is a real Austin, then. Several of the real Austin Austins had green eyes . . . but most had brown. Is she pretty or plain?"

"Awful pretty, ma'am. So pretty you'd think she was an angel."

"Oh, come now! Marshal, are you blushing?"

"No, ma'am!"

"Yes, you are. I can see that this woman made quite an impression on you. How old is she?"

"I'd say mid-twenties."

"Probably married with children. Is she fat, or thin?"

"Kinda neither, ma'am. Just about right, I'd say. Real small around the waist and—"

"My goodness, Marshal Haggen, you didn't miss much of anything, did you?"

"Well . . . "

"There you go to blushing again!"

"Ma'am, how long will it take to mend my clothes?"

"At least an hour."

"I could wait outside so's I'd not be distracting you."

"Don't bother. What kind of a dress did the lady from Austin wear?"

"A yeller one."

"A yellow dress? Hmm, now that *is* interesting. I would have thought that with reddish hair and green eyes, she'd have had better sense than to wear yellow. Green would be far more becoming, or lavender or . . . "

Festus was getting exasperated with all this chitchat. "Ma'am, I need some fresh air. I'll be back soon."

"Be about an hour, Marshal!"

"Sure thing."

And so he'd come back in an hour and the mending was done almost as good as new, which sure made it easier to pay the seamstress two whole dollars. She managed to learn a few more things about the lady named Austin from Austin, though. Like the color of her shoes and that she had not worn a bonnet or gloves, both of some apparent interest to the seamstress but not of any interest to Festus.

It was six o'clock by the time Festus had fed his new prisoner and then began his regular evening rounds. He would normally go by and poke his head into each of the northside saloons just so the boys would know the law was out and about. Then he'd stroll across the railroad tracks to the south side and check up on what was going on in the rowdier saloons and dance halls. About eight o'clock he'd end up at the Great Western Hotel, where many of the cowboys stayed and fights often took place.

Fortunately, this was turning out to be a quiet evening. Fortunate because Festus's mind was more on Miss Austin than it was on his official duties. He had been so busy hauling the drunk to jail that he'd not had time to take a backward glance and see where Miss Austin was going to stay while in Dodge City. She had told him that she was staying a few days, but . . . well, did that mean two days or ten?

Festus sure hoped it was the latter. Heck, it might even be longer! Miss Austin might even decide to *stay* in town, and wouldn't that be swell.

But anyone that pretty no doubt had a husband or at least a fiancé and he was already in Dodge City. It was really none of his business, though. On the other hand, Miss Austin had mentioned that she hoped to see him again, too.

Would a *married* woman say something that bold? After considerable deliberation, Festus decided that some married women would.

Festus couldn't figure any of it out and it was driving him crazy, so he angled back across the tracks and headed down to Railroad Avenue. With Miss Austin strong on his mind, he then walked up Chestnut Street until he came to the Wright House Hotel. This was the most likely place that Miss Austin would stay and so Festus lingered for about fifteen minutes hoping that she might be leaving for dinner alone and want some company.

"Well, hello, Marshal Haggen!"

He spun around so fast that his new boot heel caught on the edge of the boardwalk, nearly spilling him in the dirt.

"I'm sorry. Did I startle you?"

"No, ma'am."

"Clara. Any man who did what you did to protect my honor certainly ought to call me by my first name."

"All right, Clara."

"I was just taking a walk about town to get the feel for Dodge City. There's not a lot to see."

"Well, that depends on how you look at things," Festus replied. "I mean, if you live here and get to know all the nice people, it doesn't seem so small."

"I suppose that is true. I saw the Union Church and it's pretty, and also the courthouse, which is impressive for a town this small. No schoolhouse yet?"

"Not yet, but I reckon there will be before long. You see, Miss Austin—"

"Clara, remember?"

"Oh, yes, ma'am! Anyway, Dodge City is a cattle town. It was founded by buffalo hunters and bone pickers, then became a railhead for the Texas cattle drovers."

"I didn't see any cattle."

"Most of them have already been shipped," Festus explained. "We'll still get a few late herds coming up, but not many. Thing of it is, these grasslands are awful good for farming and they're slowly being fenced. More and more families are moving into Dodge, so everything is changing."

"Do the changes disappoint you?"

"No, ma'am! I mean, Miss Clara."

"Just Clara will do, if you please. Being from Texas, I've heard a lot of stories about these wild cattle towns where men are killed practically every day."

"Aw, that isn't true. Especially in Dodge City, where Matt Dillon is the regular marshal."

"Well, I have heard the stories and so I was interested in seeing them all, but of course that's impossible, for I am on my way to Colorado."

"Oh." Festus tried to hide his disappointment. "To visit your husband?"

Clara shook her head.

"Fiancé, then?"

"Why are you so curious?"

"I . . . I just like to keep up on what is happening in Dodge City."

"Even if it is personal."

"Ma'am, I'm real sorry to have asked, and—"

"Oh, it's all right! I'm going to see my older brother, Doug. He ran off to the Colorado goldfields and never returned. I'd very much like to find him."

"I sure hope you do."

"So do I." She sighed. "You see, Marshal Haggen, we have come into an unexpected inheritance."

"That's real nice!"

"Yes, it is. Have you ever received an inheritance?"

"No, and it ain't likely I will. My family comes from the hill country and most of them are real poor. I haven't done so bad, though."

"Is that a fact?"

"It sure is! I've been a-savin' money for a long, long time."

"How admirable of you! Tell me, Marshal, have you had any supper yet?"

"No, ma'am!"

"Then perhaps . . ." Clara giggled. "This is entirely too bold, but I am wondering if you . . ."

"Would like to take you to supper?"

"No, I would like to take *you* in repayment for your gallantry this afternoon."

"I couldn't allow that, ma'am. But I would be honored to treat you to a steak at Delmonico's."

Clara smiled so nice that Festus thought his knees would start knocking when she said, "Marshal, that would be lovely!"

Festus felt happy enough to sing when he extended his bent arm and Miss Clara accepted it and then away they went, just as easy and nice as anything.

The next two hours passed with the sweet swiftness of a happy dream. It turned out that Clara actually was related to Stephen Austin . . . her father was his first cousin.

"Stephen was never rich, but his memory is revered in Texas," Clara explained. "Did you know that he was tossed into a Mexico City prison when he went down to plead for more fairness and representation for the early Texas homesteaders?"

"No, I did not."

"Well, he was, and was badly mistreated. Stephen Austin was a man of great honor, like Sam Houston."

"I was told Sam Houston was no gentleman," Festus dared to say.

"Well, he was physically huge and very imposing, I've heard. Very manly and rugged. Sam Houston saved Texas by defeating that despot General Santa Anna. He is a great man and a hero."

"Matthew Dillon is pretty great himself," Festus told her.

"Who?"

"Marshal Dillon."

"But I thought you were the marshal of Dodge City."

"I am, but only while he's recovering from a broken leg . . . and a bullet wound to the neck."

"The neck?" She made a face.

"That's right."

Festus quickly told her about Waco Black, and how they'd outsmarted and then gunned him down out at the Johnson homestead.

"You *are* quite a man," Clara said, steepling her long and lovely fingers and gazing deeply into his eyes until he was so overcome with love he felt like he as drowning.

"Aw, shucks, Miss Austin, "I'm not so much of anything."

"Oh, yes you are! You risk your life every day to kill and arrest outlaws, gunfighters, and all manner of riffraff."

Festus swallowed hard. "Well," he admitted, "I just do my level best."

"Of course you do," she agreed sweetly as their last cup of coffee was served, long after the dessert of apple pie vanished. "And, if you don't mind my saying so, from what I've seen, your best is remarkable. I'm sure that you'll want to remain a marshal after Mr. Dillon returns."

Festus blinked. "I'm afraid that's not possible."

"Why?"

"Because Dodge City can only afford one marshal and that is Mr. Dillon."

"Then you'll be moving on?"

"Well, I . . . "

"Why don't you come to Colorado, which is the land of opportunity? You might even become the marshal of the town where I find my brother."

"What town would that be, Clara?"

"I'm not sure, but I think Doug disappeared somewhere in the vicinity of Goldpan Creek."

"I've heard of that town and I'm not sure it is a good place for a lady to go alone."

"Oh, I'm not entirely defenseless. I carry a derringer in my purse."

"Can you use it?"

"You bet I can! And I've heard that Goldpan Creek is high up in the mountains near a place called Pikes Peak."

"That's pretty tall, ain't it?"

"Marshal," she answered, leaning forward intently, "I've heard that Pike's Peak is so high eagles get dizzy, and have to land and walk in order to cross over the top."

"Aw, I doubt that!"

Clara giggled. "I was being ridiculous. But I have heard it is very high and very beautiful in the Rocky Mountains. I've lived most of my life around Austin and I want to be in the high, cool mountains for a while. Tell me something more about your upbringing."

Festus told Clara a few things about his rough backwoods childhood, shining them up considerably.

"You have had a very adventurous and interesting life," Clara declared. "And I'm also seeking adventure. First, I'll locate my brother to give him his inheritance and then I'll just live life to the fullest."

"I'd like to see more country, too," he blurted, surprising even himself with this revelation, because, up until this very moment, he'd thought Dodge suited him just fine.

"Is that so?"

"Maybe that's what I've been saving for all along but didn't know it."

"That could well be," Clara said. "Do you . . . well, have a lot of money?"

"About five hundred dollars in the bank. I had seven hundred but then I bought all these clothes."

"Most people spend money a lot faster than they save it," Clara told him. "Festus, what you've done says a lot and you ought to be very proud."

"I guess I am."

Festus would have talked on and on, except that it was getting late and the restaurant was ready to close. "Well," he said, getting up after paying the bill and trying not to show how he hated to spend so much money on one meal, but instead to act like he did it all the time.

"Festus, I can't thank you enough."

"I'll walk you back to the hotel, Clara . . . if you want."

"I would like that."

"Will you be leavin' pretty soon?"

"In a few days."

"Oh."

She looked closely at him. "Do you care?"

"I . . . I . . ."

"You *do* care!" She laughed and squeezed his arm. "What a sweetheart you are! You have made me feel so very welcome in Dodge City. I can't wait to write home and tell my family about you and then my brother, Ted."

"Ted?"

"I meant Doug," she quickly amended. "I only wish he could someday meet a brave and handsome man like you. I think you and . . . and Doug would become close friends."

"Miss Clara?"

"Yes?"

"Could I take you to breakfast?"

She stopped on the boardwalk, then turned and looked up into his eyes. Clara was so close that Festus started to tremble, and then she asked, "Are you sure that you can afford the time with so many troublemakers in town?"

"I'll be fine and so will Dodge City."

"In that case, would nine o'clock be agreeable? I'm not very wide-awake until that hour."

"It'd be fine." Festus gulped, doubting that he'd sleep much, with this woman fresh on his mind. "Real fine!"

"In that case, it is a date."

Festus finished escorting Miss Clara back to her hotel and then he floated on back to the jail, where the drunk was snoring. Festus pulled his chair out on the board-walk, kicked his heels up on a hitching rail, and grinned at the moon as he relived every enchanting moment he'd shared with Miss Clara Austin.

My, oh my, he thought, feeling almost giddy with infatuation, *I wonder if I could get a job as marshal of Goldpan Creek or one of them surrounding gold-mining towns up in the Rocky Mountains.*

CHAPTER

14

"Matt?"

He had been dozing through the warm afternoon when Kitty unlocked the door and found him stretched out on a sofa with a book of poems resting in his huge hands.

"Yeah?" Matt tried to rouse himself awake instantly but was less than successful.

"Did you hear about Festus?"

"Is he all right? Does he need—"

"Take it easy," Kitty told him. "Festus is just fine and doesn't need anything. In fact, I think he might have found *everything* he needs, judging from the dreamy expression on his face."

Matt pushed himself into a sitting position and the book of poetry slid forgotten to the floor. He knuckled sleep from his eyes. "What time is it?"

"About three o'clock. Long afternoon nap."

"I've got to start moving around more and sleeping

less," Matt said. "I'm starting to act and feel like an old man ready for the rocking chair."

Kitty sat down next to him. "I wouldn't be too worried about that. You've already worked and lived hard enough for three normal men. But what I wanted to tell you about was Festus and Clara."

"Clara who?"

"Miss Clara Austin from Austin."

Matt yawned. "Kitty, why don't you start from the beginning and tell me what this Clara business is all about?"

"Festus is smitten!" Kitty exclaimed, unable to contain her excitement. "Miss Austin arrived by stagecoach yesterday and was set upon by some drunken lout. Festus jumped in and took care of the problem, arresting and jailing the man. I guess the young lady was quite impressed, because they went out for supper last night and then breakfast again this morning."

"Festus went to a restaurant for two meals in a row?"

"That's right! He took Miss Austin to Delmonico's last night. Can you imagine him spending money like that for any other reason than love?"

Matt had to grin. "No."

"They were seen walking arm in arm last evening and I heard that Delmonico's had to practically throw them out the door, because they were having so much fun that they didn't want to leave at closing time. And then, just this morning, Al at the Bonnie Bee Café said that the couple couldn't keep their eyes off each other and hardly touched a bite of food."

Matt was coming awake now. "I can't believe that Festus is acting like this."

"Doc told me to tell you he said so."

"Said what?"

"That we were dealing with an entirely new Festus; one that would be a continual surprise."

"What kind of woman is Miss Austin?"

"She's quite attractive. All my girls are jealous."

"Of Miss Austin?"

"That's right. I didn't tell you this, but there are at least three of my girls that have sort of . . . well, fallen for Festus."

Matt shook his head back and forth. "I don't believe what I'm hearing."

"Believe it or not, the new Festus is now considered to be quite a marriage prize. He has definitely become one of Dodge City's most eligible bachelors."

"And all because he's cleaned up and bought a nice set of clothes?"

"Of course not! Overnight, our friend has changed his entire demeanor."

"His what?"

"His *attitude* has changed," Kitty said. "He's gotten confident . . . but not arrogant or cocky. Festus is simply a changed man, and one that the women like much better."

Matt frowned. "Kitty, there is still some cold coffee in the pot over on the stove. Would you please pour me a cup?"

"Sure." She brought it back to him moments later with a smile and said, "You just have to see them together."

"Festus and Miss Austin?"

"Who else are we talking about?"

"That fries it," Matt said, kicking off the bedcovers. "Doc or no Doc, I'm getting out the crutches and hobbling over to the office before my mind and body turn into corn mush."

"Well, that won't do. I heard what Doc said about your legbone and—"

"Then I'll hire a couple of men to carry me!" Matt lowered his voice. "I'm sorry for losing my temper and yelling, Kitty. It has nothing to do with you and everything to do with the way things are going."

"What's wrong with the way things are going in

Dodge? Everyone but you seems satisfied with the job Festus is doing."

"I'm satisfied. It's just that, well, I'm also worried."

"About Festus getting killed doing his duty?"

"Yeah, but even more about what will happen when he has to hand over his badge and become a deputy again."

"Ah, now I see. And you're right to be worried. I know that Doc shares that concern. It will be hard on Festus to play second fiddle again."

"I'm beginning to think so."

"But . . . but perhaps the town council will agree to honor Festus because of the way he filled in while you were down. They could present him with a nicer badge and a new title, along with a long-overdue pay raise."

"You mean give him a title such as 'assistant marshal'?"

"Exactly!"

"That's a fine idea, Kitty. But I'm not too optimistic they'll give him a raise."

"Why not? He's earned it."

"Sure he has, but—"

"No buts about it," Kitty said. "Festus is underpaid and so are you."

"Name me a marshal who isn't," Matt said. "And we both know that the town council is extremely tightfisted."

"Yes, but Dodge City is growing so that you and Festus have to work harder every year."

"It's getting to be impossible," Matt said in agreement. "I really need another deputy, at least a part-time one that Festus could help supervise."

"I'll talk to the council members one by one when they come in for a drink. I'll remind them that neither you nor Festus has had a decent raise in . . . in how awfully long?"

"Almost two years. And prices are going up all over town."

"Of course they are. Matt, I'll threaten to raise the price of their drinks if they don't come around with a couple of pay raises for you and Festus."

"Thanks, Kitty. Now, will you bring me my crutches?"

"I'm not sure that I ought to do this."

Matt winked. "Don't make me have to hop one-legged over there. At my age, it wouldn't be all that pretty."

Kitty laughed and got the crutches and held them while Matt buckled on his gun belt.

"You really think you need to pack a six-gun?"

"I sure do," Matt replied with conviction. "A lawman makes enemies and most of the ones I've made wouldn't hesitate to gun me down . . . even on a pair of crutches. It's not likely, but I intend to play it safe."

Kitty handed him the crutches and went to open the door, saying, "You've *never* played it safe and you never will. My guess is that your biggest threat out there is running into Doc."

It was Matt's turn to chuckle as he made his way to the door. "If we have the bad luck to run into him on the way to the jail, please help defend me."

"Not a chance!"

"Come on, Kitty," he said, pretending desperation as they reached the street. "Friends have to stick together."

"We've been stuck together," she replied, winking. "But I'm not facing Doc's wrath. This is your idea and yours alone."

Matt just grunted. He'd forgotten his darned hat and it was too much trouble to return to the house, so he just kept going while hoping not to meet Doc. Luck was with him, and when he reached the jail, Matt went inside and was greeted by their new prisoner.

"Hey, Dillon, you ain't lookin' too damned good these days!" the rumpled young man called from his cell. "Too bad."

"Shut up, Junior," Kitty warned. "Even with no legs, he'd still be twice the man that you'll ever be."

"You ought to know!"

Matt glared at their mouthy prisoner. "I heard you

caused some trouble yesterday when the stage from Texas arrived. How long have you been in Dodge City?"

"Long enough to know that I want *out* of Dodge just as quick as possible."

"You'll be leaving as soon as the judge levies a fine for being drunk and disorderly."

"How much will that cost me?"

"Probably five dollars. Ten, if I tell him how rude and disrespectful you are toward ladies."

The prisoner took a deep breath and expelled it slowly. He mussed his brown hair and forced a weak grin. "Miss Kitty, I *am* sorry for my disgraceful behavior. I was taught better by my mother and am ashamed of myself. I sure hope you will accept my most humble apology."

Kitty's expression said that she didn't believe a word of what he'd said, but she answered, "All right, Junior, you're forgiven."

"I sure hope so, because I only got seven dollars to my name and I don't want to leave town dead broke."

"If you keep behaving yourself," Matt told him, "you'll get the five-dollar fine. Where is Marshal Haggen?"

"Who knows?" the prisoner responded, raising his hands palms up. "I ain't seen much of him since I sobered up this morning. I can tell you he has hitched his wagon to an awful pretty young woman."

"So I've heard."

Matt sat down at this desk, looking at the stack of new WANTED posters and correspondence that was piling up in his absence.

"I'm leaving," Kitty told him. "You look as if you've got business on your mind."

"I do. And thanks."

"Sure, but don't you dare tell Doc I had anything to do with your getting out on the town again."

"I won't."

When Kitty was gone, Matt attended to his neglected paperwork. There were several local letters to answer as well as the usual notice of town meetings and obligations that he was expected to attend. There were also two letters from men inquiring about filling in for Matt as marshal while he was recovering from his leg injury. Both men sounded qualified, especially the one from a former longtime constable of a small farming settlement named Grover, located in eastern Colorado. His name was Jack Casey and he said he'd turned part-time farmer, but it wasn't working out and he'd like to get back into law.

Matt set Jack's letter aside where it would not get pitched or forgotten. He would write to the man and explain that there might be a part-time opening in Dodge City next spring when the cattle started arriving again and things got crazy because of all the wild Texas cowboys.

He was about to go over the WANTED posters when he looked out the front window and saw Festus standing outside the door with Miss Clara Austin. *My,* he thought, *she is a looker!*

Festus touched the young woman's arm in a way that a man does when he feels more than just friendship or concern. Then he waved good-bye and came inside. Matt's presence startled him and the wide smile on his freshly shaven face was instantly replaced with a frown.

"Matthew, what are you doin' here?"

"I'm going over some paperwork."

"But Doc said—"

"I know what he said. But I was going crazy and had to get out and see what was going on here."

"Everything is under control." Festus scowled at the cell and their prisoner. "That fella is the only problem I've had since I've seen you last. He seems to have settled down and regained his good sense."

"Thanks for the fine compliment, Marshal Haggen!"

"You're welcome, I guess."

"So when can I pay the five dollars to the judge and be on my way?"

"Who told you it was only going to be five dollars?"

"He did," the prisoner answered, pointing at Matt. "Dillon said that if I was respectful, that would be the fine."

"Well, listen here now," Festus replied. "You just never know what kind of a fine the judge will decide upon. It sort of depends on the particular mood he happens to be in when you're brought before him in court."

"Aw, come on! I am sorry and I just want to leave town. Why can't I pay you and be set free right now?"

" 'Cause that just ain't the way we do things in Dodge City. Ain't that right, Matthew?"

"That's right, Marshal. We operate according to the laws of Dodge City and Kansas and bend them for no man."

"See there," Festus crowed. "We're professional."

"Great to hear that," the prisoner said, voice dripping with cynicism.

Matt studied the first WANTED poster and then thumbed through the rest. He'd seen none of the men, but would keep looking the posters over every day until they were all well etched in his memory. It was a practice that had resulted in numerous arrests in the past and might well have saved his life.

"Festus," he said, when the man brought him some coffee, "I couldn't help but see that woman you were with outside. She's very pretty."

"She is that, all right!" Festus exclaimed. "Her name is Miss Clara Austin and she's from Austin."

Festus told Matthew about how she was just passing through Dodge City on her way to the Colorado goldfields up in the Rocky Mountains. He ended by saying, "I'm a-hopin' she decides to stay here awhile before leavin'."

"I suspect that you are hoping she *never* leaves," Matt said, studying his deputy closely. "At least, that's the word that I'm hearing around town."

"Matthew, have folks already started a-waggin' their tongues about me and Miss Clara?"

"Well, of course. This is a small town and you're the marshal now and so people are watching you closely. It comes with the territory."

"Well, I do declare! Ain't people got themselves anything better to do than worry about other people's doin's?"

"I guess not."

"Hmmph! People need to get themselves something more important to yap their traps about."

"Dodge City is still a small town and small towns don't have many secrets. Now, you ought to have figured that out by yourself."

"Maybe so, but—"

Festus was cut off by their prisoner, who yelled, "Hey, Marshal Haggen, if you don't want to marry her, say the word and I will instead!"

"Shut up!" Festus snapped. "She ain't interested in marryin' nobody until she finds her brother up near Gold-pan Creek. Maybe even after that she won't marry. I don't know nothing about it, myself."

If they had been alone, Matt would have laughed outright at how sensitive Festus was on this tender subject. But because they did have a prisoner, he managed to keep a straight face and just ask a few simple questions about the young lady, which Festus quickly answered.

"Miss Austin sounds like a fine person," Matt concluded. "But why would a young woman like that go off alone to find her brother?"

Festus's eyebrows shot upward. "What do you mean?"

"Why didn't her father go to find his wayward son? Or some other relative? Seems to me that she's taking a risk."

116

"I told her the same thing," Festus replied. "I hear those mining camps are wilder than wet weasels. But Clara said she would be all right. She carries a derringer and says she knows how to use it. I believe her, too. Miss Austin is not a fainthearted woman."

"Apparently not."

"I admire her, Matthew. She's taken the bull by the horns and set out to find that brother and give him his part of their inheritance."

"I see. What's his name?"

"Ted . . . no, Doug. Doug Austin."

"Maybe you could help her by sending a telegram to Goldpan Creek and asking that it be given to the marshal or whoever is the law there. He might have heard of Clara's brother and then he could tell him to come to Dodge City and pick up his inheritance."

"Say, now! That is a fine idea!" Festus jumped up and ran for the door as if the office was on fire. "I'll send that telegram and be right back! Clara is sure going to be surprised!"

The door slammed hard enough to rattle the windows and Matt shook his head.

"Sure must be nice to be in love," their prisoner said with a cluck of his tongue. "You ever been in love, Dillon?"

"That's none of your affair."

"I guess not. But I was in love once."

Matt looked up from his paperwork. "Is that right?"

"Her name was Calico."

"An Indian girl?"

"No, she was my first cat."

"Shut up," Matt snapped at the grinning fool as he picked up his pen and began to answer his correspondence.

CHAPTER

15

"Festus," Clara said quietly, "I can't stay here in Dodge City any longer. I've already stayed too long . . . because of you."

"Ten days and a couple hours ain't all that long. And I'm worried about you going up into those wild Colorado mining towns all by yourself."

"I have to find my brother, Doug."

"Yeah, but . . . but it ain't safe for a lady to travel alone in those kind of places."

They were sitting beside the banks of the Arkansas River, just watching the passing of billowy white clouds and slow-moving water.

"Listen," Festus said, "I admire you for wanting to find your brother, but what if he don't want to be found?"

She looked sharply at him. "What is that supposed to mean?"

"Well," Festus said, choosing his words carefully and not wanting to hurt her feelings any, "Doug ain't written any letters or tried in any way to contact you, has he?"

"No, but he isn't the kind that would unless he had some kind of good news. I expect that Doug is not doing well. Festus, he might even be sick or dying!"

"Or already dead," Festus dared to say.

"Festus!"

"I'm sorry, Clara, but it's just that I don't think you should risk your life to find a man that maybe don't even want to be found."

"We have an inheritance. It's not large. Just over four thousand dollars, but half belongs to Doug and he might need it badly." Tears filled her eyes. "I sure will miss you."

"And I'll miss you," Festus replied, feeling like someone had kicked him in the stomach. "If Matthew wasn't laid up and needing me so much, I'd . . . well, never mind."

"You'd what?"

"I'd tag along with you to Goldpan Creek and help you find your brother and make sure that nothing went wrong."

She leaned close. Festus's heart started skipping and he put his arm across Clara's shoulders, then drew her to him and kissed her lips. Kissed 'em for a long, lingering moment that left them both breathless.

Clara came to her feet. "I'd better get back to the hotel and start packing."

"What's your hurry? The train for Pueblo don't leave until tomorrow morning."

"Let's not make this any harder than it needs to be," she told him as she started on the path back to town.

Festus jumped up and chased after her, but he didn't know what to say and feared that words would only make things worse. So, with his hands in his pants pockets and his hat tipped low, he silently followed her to the hotel.

"I think we ought to say good-bye right now," Clara told him with a tremor in her voice. "The Atchison, Topeka and the Santa Fe arrives tomorrow at ten o'clock and it will be headed for Pueblo one hour later."

Festus struggled for words. "I . . . I was hopin' to take you out one more time and—"

"It's too painful. You have a good life here, with many wonderful friends. I can tell that you are admired and respected."

"It used to seem thataway," he heard himself tell her, "before you."

"Stop." Clara gently placed a forefinger on his lips. "I don't know what will happen when I get to Colorado, but I'm sure that I'll be fine."

"Won't you at least be coming back through Dodge on your way home to Austin?"

"I don't know."

Clara picked up a stone and threw it into the slow-moving river. They both watched the ripples fade out of sight.

"Like I told you before," she continued, "I've always wanted to live in mountains. I yearn to see new vistas, Festus. I don't want to spend my whole life in Austin, Texas."

"Sure, but—"

"I will miss you very, very much."

Festus wanted to tell her that he would miss her, too, but his throat was swelling shut. So he just shuffled his new boots in the dust, took off his hat, and nodded good-bye. Just like that, and his life seemed like a train wreck; the bright sun faded, the clouds turned gray, and the air felt cold. Miss Clara Austin was gone and so was the joy in his life.

He was in a daze when he reached town. "Afternoon, Marshal," someone called, but Festus scarcely heard them and did not trust his voice to return the greeting. So he turned and walked away, feeling dead inside.

Festus wasn't a hard-drinking man, but that evening he got stinking drunk down by the riverbank where he and Clara had laughed and spent so many happy hours. He slept by the Arkansas and woke up late, knowing that he had a job to do and not much caring to do it.

The day before, Judge Brooker had fined and released his prisoner, so there was no real need to return to the office. Festus felt so awful he decided to stay out of sight until after Clara's train was gone.

He removed his clothes and went for a swim. It cleared his head some and he stretched out on the grass. At ten o'clock, he heard the steam whistle of the train blasting as it rolled into Dodge. One hour later and with his heart feeling like it had been stomped on by a horse, Festus heard the train whistle again, announcing its departure.

Only then did he dress and return to town. Those who saw him were shocked by his haggard appearance. His new suit was soiled, his black boots caked with river mud, his hair mussed, and his jowls unshaven. Even worse in appearance were his eyes, which were not only bloodshot, but reflected a yawning inner emptiness.

"Holy mackerel, Marshal!" Skinny Sally exclaimed when she met him nearing the office. "What happened to *you* all of a sudden?"

"Nothing," he muttered.

Sally fell in walking beside him. "I can't believe how far you've fallen since yesterday. Did you lose a friend or . . . oh, I get it! Miss Austin got on the westbound train for Colorado."

"That's right. Now, Sally, I'd appreciate it if you'd just leave me alone."

"I will," she said, "but I don't think being alone is what you need. In fact, I think that is the very *last* thing you need. Why don't you come over to my crib and sleep it off. Maybe later, if you're feeling good, I could find a way to take your mind off that Texas girl."

"Thanks, but no thanks."

"Well, at least I tried, Marshal."

Festus entered his office and collapsed in his desk chair. He laid his head down on his muscular forearms and had himself a good, hard cry. Afterward he made a pot of coffee and drank it while gazing at a flyspeck on the wall.

"Festus?"

"Aw, Doc, go away!"

"My gawd, man, what is the matter with you?"

"I just need to be left alone."

"No you don't. Miss Austin left town today, didn't she?"

"Yep."

"Festus, you can't take it so hard. There will be other women."

"I don't want any other women. Clara is the one I'll always love."

"Oh, bosh! I'll admit she was pretty, intelligent, and nice. And I can see how you'd fall hard. But there are others, and you're now considered a 'catch' by many young women. So go over to Butterworth's barbershop and get a bath, a fresh shave, and a haircut. Do those things and I guarantee that you'll start feeling better again."

"Go away, Doc!"

"You look like hell, Festus. I mean it!"

When Festus didn't even glance at him, Doc poured himself a cup of coffee and sat down at Matt's desk, trying to think of something helpful to say.

"Listen, I got my heart broken a couple of times when I was your age and it always healed. Yours will, too, but getting drunk and wanting to be alone is the *worst* thing you should do. You need to clean up, get a woman, and—"

"Doc, get out of here!"

Doc headed for the door, wagging his forefinger and saying, "Pull yourself together! You're the marshal of Dodge City and people are depending on you to keep the peace. I'm depending on you, Kitty is depending on you, and Matt swore that you were man enough to hold this office while he was laid up."

He filled his corncob pipe, glaring at Festus, and his parting words were, "Are you going to make a fool out of Matt? Is that what you intend to do to all your friends that told the doubters you could handle the badge?"

Finally, Festus looked up. His eyes were shiny with

tears and he managed to say, "In a while I'll get cleaned up again and I'll be all right. Don't worry, Doc. I won't never let you and my other special friends down."

Doc's voice softened. "Look, I'm a physician and I deal with ailments, but I know that the heartache you're feeling is as sharp as any physical pain. If I could prescribe a pill or a potion, something to ease your suffering, I'd do it in a moment. But . . . I can't. Getting drunk won't help, it'll make things worse. I can only tell you from experience that you have to get on with the business of life. Your life and your business is very important."

"Thanks, Doc."

"Okay, then," he said, "take care, and get something to eat."

"I will."

When Doc left, he went over to see Matt and came right to the point. "Festus looks like a broken man. I think you need to go over and talk to him."

"What about your orders to stay—"

"Hang my orders! You've been sneaking out so much behind my back already that it don't matter none anyway. How does the leg feel?"

"Great. Swelling is gone."

"Let me be the judge of that. Lift that pant leg."

Doc inspected the broken leg with a series of unintelligible grunts.

"What do you think, Doc?"

"I think you've got a mighty strong legbone that's healing in spite of what you've been up to."

"Then I'm going to the office and I'm not using them damned crutches anymore."

"What!"

"I'll use a cane and go slow."

Doc acted like he wanted to object, but he didn't. Instead, he muttered, "Look after Festus. Maybe you could stay at the jail and sleep on the cot in the cell for the next week or two until you can throw away the crutch."

"I'll do that," Matt promised as he pulled on his vest and then strapped on his cartridge belt and holster. He found his hat and then the cane he'd already taken to using. "Don't worry, I'll be fine."

"I'm a lot more worried about Festus now than I am about you. What ails him I can't treat."

"Festus is strong," Matt said. "He'll survive."

"I don't know about that. First he loses the girl he loves, next he loses his position as town marshal and returns to being a nobody."

"A 'nobody'!" Matt shook his head angrily. "Doc, you know better than to say that about Festus. He was valuable before I got hurt and he'll be the same after I return."

"*I* know that. *You* know that and so does Kitty. But will Festus?"

Matt nodded with understanding. "I'll be his deputy for the next week or two."

"That might help. Good luck, Matt. He looks terrible."

Matt hurried as fast as he could over to the office to find his friend staring at the ceiling.

"All right," he boomed, "I'm going to become your deputy and live here. Doc says my leg has healed enough that I can hobble around on a cane. So fill me in on what is going on, Marshal Haggen."

In the days that followed, Festus got a haircut, a shave, and a bath but Matt knew that there was a lot missing that had been there before. It was . . . well, the man's spirit seemed to be broken. It was like he was sleepwalking through a bad dream. Festus put in the hours, he made his rounds on time, but Matt had the feeling that he neither saw nor heard anything.

"Kitty," Matt confided one hot afternoon, "I'm scared to death that someone is going to hurt Festus. Sooner or later they'll discover he's hollow inside and they'll hurt, if not kill him outright."

"It's that serious?"

"It is," Matt replied. "Festus has lost his passion for being a lawman. If he wasn't such a close friend and I didn't need him so much, I'd send him packing for his own darned good!"

"Then that's what you need to do."

"I can't," Matt told her. "I'm not yet physically able to make the rounds and do the job."

"Then hire someone else! Matt, if the town council won't back you up on this, then I'll pay the new man's salary for a month or two until things get sorted out."

"You'd do that?"

"Of course I would! Why, since you've just told me this, I'm already worried sick about Festus getting jumped or shot. Do you have someone in mind that could fill in for Festus?"

"There's a man . . . and I don't know a thing about him other than he's farming at a little settlement in eastern Colorado named Grover. Anyway, he wrote saying he doesn't want to farm anymore and has constable experience."

"I've been through Grover. It isn't much more than a whistle-stop on the railroad line. A water tower, a few buildings, and that's all, other than scattered homesteads. What is this man's name?"

"Jack Casey. I expect he's an older fella."

"Older might be good," Kitty told him. "You don't want some young fire-eater to step in, and besides you'd have to tell him that he'd only have the job until Festus wants it back."

"That's right, or that he would have to go part-time. An older man might go for that."

"Let's get ahold of him, Matt."

"I could send a message on the train."

"No," Kitty said. "A message could get lost. Besides, we need someone in a hurry!"

"So what—"

"I'll go find Casey. If he can walk and talk and shoot, I'll tell him I have the authority to hire him."

"I don't know about that."

"I do. Remember that most of the town council patronize my saloon. I wield a lot more influence than you might imagine."

Matt nodded, and looking into Kitty's green eyes, he knew that she was telling him for the first time just how important she was in the politics of Dodge City.

"All right. A train leaves tomorrow."

"I'll be on it and be back within three or four days. Sam will be in charge of the Long Branch as usual."

"Fine, but if Jack Casey doesn't seem to fit the bill, don't hire him. A bad deputy is even worse than no deputy."

"Which is what you have now."

"No, *I'm* the deputy now, remember?"

"Whatever you say, but I don't have to believe it, do I?"

"No," Matt told her, "I guess you don't have to do anything you don't want to do."

"You got that right," Kitty said with a wink.

He watched her get up and walk away, and the thought occurred to him that even if he asked, Kitty might not be willing to marry him. And why should she? Kitty had power, money, and was far more popular than he would ever be.

As Matt slowly hobbled back to the office, Doc intercepted him. "What's going on?"

"I'm going to fire Festus."

"You can't do that! He's the marshal now."

"I know." Matt frowned. "Doc, he's just walking death. But you are right. I have no authority to fire him. So I'll just *ask* him to resign."

"Will he?"

"I'm sure of it," Matt answered. "Festus needs to go find Miss Austin and decide if they ought to get married or not."

"What if she turns him down?"

"Then at least he'll know, which will be better than not knowing."

"That's true," Doc mused aloud. "All right, mind if I come along and help ease his pain?"

"Of course not."

So they headed slowly down the street toward a show-down with Marshal Festus.

CHAPTER

16

"Festus," Matt said in greeting as they entered his office, "how are you?"

The marshal looked up from his desk. "Fine, Matthew. Everything is under control."

But Doc shook his head as he took a chair. "You never were much of a liar. Your thoughts are written all over your homely mug."

"Doc, I ain't in no mood for your teasin' today."

"All right, I'll behave. But Matt has something important that he needs to talk about and maybe I can help."

Festus turned to Matt. "Have I done something wrong, Matthew?"

"Nothing at all."

"Well, then why do you fellers look so glum?"

"We're sad because you are sad," Matt replied. "We know how much you cared about Miss Austin."

"Well, Clara must not have cared as much about me because she left on that westbound train."

"She left because she had to find her brother," Doc reminded him.

"Yeah, but . . . well, I just don't know."

"You're in love with her," Matt said flatly. "Or at least, you think you are."

"I can't deny it, Matthew. That girl broke my heart. I had a puppy once that got tromped flatter than a horned toad and I thought my poor little heart would break. But this is a whole lot worse!"

"Festus," Matt said, "I don't want you to get the wrong idea, but I think you should turn in your badge and go find Miss Austin in Colorado."

Festus sat up straight, his face transformed from sadness to disbelief. "I'd never leave you in a fix! I can't do that!"

"Sure you can. I've even hired a temporary replacement to help out while you're gone." It wasn't exactly the truth, but Matt could see it needed saying or Festus simply wouldn't agree.

"Who?"

"His name is Jack Casey and he farms over in eastern Colorado. He's a fine man about my age with lots of experience."

"How come he ain't a marshal anymore?"

"He thought he'd try dry-land farming but he doesn't like it and wants back in law."

Festus glanced at Doc. "Do you think Matthew can get along without me while I go to Colorado? I sure wouldn't want anything to go wrong with his leg healin' proper."

"I think it will be all right," Doc replied. "We've talked it over, and as you can see, Matt is getting along pretty well with a cane."

Festus couldn't hide his growing excitement. "Well, I'd have to wait until this Casey fella arrives."

"No, you won't," Matt told him. "Jack Casey will be along any day now and I've got other friends who can back me up. Besides, there are only a few Texas cowboys left in Dodge and they're about to leave for home. I'll be fine."

"Are you sure?"

Doc frowned. "He's said he's sure and so did I. Now the train heads out tomorrow morning and you need to be on it. Is that clearly understood?"

"Yes, sir!"

Festus jumped up, a changed man. He actually did a little jig and then he strode over to the mirror, studied himself for a moment, and declared, "I'll get a shave, bath, and haircut this very afternoon! Get my boots shined, my shirt and suit cleaned and pressed. I'm not lookin' too spiffy right now, but I will be when I find my Clara!"

"Listen," Doc said, "you have to understand that things don't always work out the way you want or think they should . . . especially in love."

The marshal's smile melted. "Doc, are you trying to tell me that she might not marry me even after she finds her brother?"

"That's right. Women change their minds fast. Some are . . . and I mean no offense, but they are damned fickle."

"Not Miss Austin," Festus said, chin jutting out. "She loves me and only left because of a sense of duty to poor Doug."

"That's probably true, but you have to be ready in case things still don't work out."

Matt cleared his throat. "Didn't you tell me that the young woman wanted to live in the Rocky Mountains?"

"Yeah, but—"

"Then you may have to choose between coming back as a deputy and staying in the mountains and finding some other line of work, or maybe a marshal's job in a mining town."

"I guess that's true enough. Hadn't thought of it until now. I sure would hate to—"

"Just let it unfold," Matthew advised. "Most often things work out for the best either way."

"I suppose."

"Of course they do," Doc said. "Besides, what do you really know about Miss Austin, other than that she has a brother and comes from Austin?"

"She has an inheritance."

"That's good, but, my friend, it hardly qualifies as knowing her past well enough to predict how she might be as a future wife."

"She's a real good woman, Doc."

"I know that, but—"

"And she loves me."

"I'm sure that's true, but there are other things you have to consider."

Festus squinted suspiciously. "Like what?"

"Well, does she like kids, for example?"

"I don't know. I expect so."

"Would she like to have a family?"

"Doc, you're a-gettin' way ahead of things! I ain't got no ring and I ain't even had time to propose yet."

"Seems to me that you're acting like a lovesick calf and hardly know a thing about this young lady, other than that she comes from Texas, has a brother, and wants to live in the mountains. That doesn't seem like enough to me, Festus."

"It is for me!"

"Matt, talk some sense into him."

But Matt shook his head. "When it comes to love, since when does sense matter? Festus will find out all these things in time."

"I ain't so sure," Doc groused.

"Well, I will, you cantankerous old goat!"

Anger flared in Doc's eyes and Festus already had his dander up, so Matt stepped between the pair. "Doc, why don't you go for a walk? Festus and I have a few things to clear up before he starts getting ready to leave for Colorado on tomorrow's train."

"Sure will," Doc snapped. "I just hate to see him act like a lovesick—"

"That's enough," Matt said, escorting the feisty physician out the door.

"Matthew, he sure gets under my skin."

"Don't let Doc upset you. He means well and you know what a great friend he is to all of us."

"Yeah, I do," Festus admitted. "When Waco Black wanted to brace me, it was Doc and Kitty that changed his mind with their guns. You don't find friends like them every day."

"You sure don't," Matt agreed. "Now, why don't you show me what I have to do in the paperwork department after you leave?"

"I'm afraid I'm not good at that," Festus admitted, "and I've sort of let it pile up."

"No problem. The more I sit for the next few days the better off I'll be."

"Are you really sure that this Jack Casey fella will do a good job until I—"

"Yes, I am," Matt interrupted. "Now show me what needs to be done and then go get yourself ready for leaving tomorrow."

"Yes, sir."

Later that evening Matt and Kitty met for a drink in her saloon and sat at their usual private table. The talk, of course, was all about Festus and what he might find out when he located Miss Austin.

"Kitty, what kind of woman is she?"

"From what little I've seen, Clara Austin is exactly what she says she is," Kitty replied. "I was impressed."

"So was I, but you have to admit that she never said much of anything about her past. Nothing about her father or mother. Nothing about what she did or they did.

Just some vague reference to being related to Stephen Austin."

Kitty leaned forward. "Do you think she might be hiding something?"

"It's possible," Matt said without hesitation. "I think she has very cleverly avoided any reference to her past. And, frankly, I'm a little worried about what surprises might be in store for Festus."

"Hmm," Kitty mused. "Maybe you're right. The young lady was so wholesome and charming that you just naturally assume that she has a clean conscience and a reputable past."

"And I hope that she does. But I wish that I could warn Festus to just . . . well, just be a little careful until he finds out more about her past."

"He's too lovesick to listen, isn't he?"

"Kitty, he's ready to marry Clara the minute they are together again. Now, I'm all for Festus getting married and even having a family . . . if that is what will make him happy . . . but he is awfully naive and I don't want him tricked or taken advantage of in some way we haven't yet figured."

"I agree. Festus hasn't ever had much to do with women. Then he cleaned up to become town marshal and suddenly he's a prize. If I hadn't seen it with my own eyes I would never have believed it could happen."

"Me neither." Matt sipped at his beer. "We have a problem about you getting on the same train as Festus tomorrow."

"What do you mean?"

"I told Festus that Jack Casey was hired and on his way to Dodge City."

"Matt!"

"I had no choice. Festus would never go without being sure that I had some backup help on the way to town."

"That does pose a problem since we haven't even seen Jack Casey."

"It sure does. Perhaps you should wait a couple of days until the next train."

"I think that is a very bad idea," Kitty told him in no uncertain terms. "You need a deputy right now. I'll just wait until Festus has boarded, then I'll dash out and get into another car. With luck, he'll never even know that I am also aboard and headed for Colorado."

"But what if he sees you get on or he comes through your car and there you are?"

Kitty frowned in thought. "In that case," she decided, "I'll just lie like you did. I'll tell him I have a friend or some business in Grover."

"I'm not sure that he'll believe that."

"It won't matter," Kitty said with assurance. "Festus is so smitten that he'll just go on to Colorado and find that girl anyway."

Matt nodded. "I'm sure you're right."

"It's settled, then," Kitty said. "Why don't we go out and have something good to eat like a steak?"

"Suits me. I'm the marshal of Dodge City again and that means that I'm back on marshal's pay."

"Which isn't much."

"No," Matt agreed, "but you are going to twist a few arms and get Festus and me a raise. Remember?"

"I'm working on it."

"Good," he said, pushing up from the table and grabbing his cane. "The sooner the better."

"Matt?"

"Yeah?"

"What if Festus does marry Clara Austin and she won't leave the mountains?"

"Then I'll miss him as bad as I missed Chester when he left," Matt replied. "But I'll find another deputy and friend. Maybe even Jack Casey."

"Maybe," Kitty said, "but let's hope it doesn't come to that. I'd miss Festus something awful."

"We all would, especially Doc."

Kitty agreed as they headed out to get something to eat. She would insist upon paying for dinner. She had the money and . . . well, she'd let Matt treat when he'd paid off Doc and got his raise. It didn't matter a whole lot either way.

CHAPTER

17

"All aboard!" the conductor shouted. "Last call for all aboard!"

"Kitty, you'd better get on right now," Matt suggested as they stood hidden behind the train depot. "Festus went up ahead, so you can go back to one of the rear cars."

Doc agreed. "I'm sure that Festus is so excited he won't have a clue as to who is on this train. Why, President Grover Cleveland himself could be sitting beside our boy and I doubt he'd take notice."

"All right," Kitty said, kissing them each on the cheek and then turning to go, "I'll be back with Jack Casey just as soon as I can!"

"Don't bring him if he isn't right for the job!" Matt yelled. "The last thing I need is . . ."

Kitty didn't hear the last thing that Matt said because his words were drowned out by the shriek of the steam whistle. She just had time to jump on board as the train jerked forward and began rolling westward.

The conductor steadied her with his hand. "Your ticket, ma'am."

Kitty gave the man her ticket. He was white-haired with a long handlebar mustache tinted slightly orange from the brand of tobacco he chewed. Adjusting his spectacles, the uniformed conductor studied the ticket, then Kitty.

"Is something wrong?" she asked.

"Well, it says here that you are going to Grover, Colorado."

"That's right."

The conductor frowned. "Ma'am, you ain't dressed for Grover."

"What do you mean?"

"I mean there ain't nothing there but a general store, a loading dock for cattle, and a water tank. A lady dressed like you just would be lost."

Kitty smiled. "I appreciate your concern. But I am definitely getting off at Grover. Have you ever heard of a homesteader named Jack Casey?"

"No, ma'am. Should I have?"

"I guess not."

"Does he own that general store where there's always trouble?"

"No." Kitty started to leave, then stopped and asked, "What kind of trouble?"

"Just fights, ma'am. The place has a rough reputation. Is someone going to meet you in Grover?"

"No."

"Then what are you going to do there?"

"I'm looking for Jack Casey."

The conductor smiled politely. "Good luck," he said, punching her ticket and moving down the aisle.

Kitty had been to Colorado several times but that was before the recently completed railroad line to Pueblo, when you had to take a stage. Now, as before, they would follow the Arkansas River through rolling hills that she imagined had once been the home of the Indian and the buffalo, but that were now filling up with cattle and homesteaders. Their little shacks and sod houses dotted the vast prairie, and Kitty wondered how a woman could keep her sanity in such a lonesome land.

Perhaps they socialized but Kitty still thought it would be a hard life. She could see plots of tilled ground being dry-land-farmed with wheat and corn. It had been unusually dry the last few seasons. A few of the homesteads had trees and flowers planted, but because water was at a premium and often had to be hauled from the Arkansas, mostly Kitty saw crops and a smattering of livestock.

She was lost in her own reflections about life in general, and the life of these hardy people in particular, when an unsavory-looking young man reeking of liquor tapped her on the shoulder. "Howdy, ma'am, mind if I sit beside you?"

"As a matter of fact, I do," Kitty answered, not caring for his looks or smell. "There are plenty of other empty seats."

His eyes flashed with anger. "Well, you sure are the uppity one! Who do you think you are, anyway?"

"I'm someone that you do not want to trouble."

"You ain't so pretty as you think." He sneered. "I'm twenty-two and I'll bet you're old enough to be my mother!"

"Your mother obviously never taught you any manners. Now leave me alone."

"You don't own that empty seat. Maybe I'll just sit next to you whether you like it or not."

"That would be a mistake."

"Why?"

"I'd have to call the conductor and he might toss you off this train in the middle of nowhere."

"That white-haired old man couldn't toss me noplace!"

Kitty glared at the intruder. "Why don't you just go sit down someplace else and be a good little boy?"

"You callin' me a 'boy'?"

"I'm being charitable."

"Huh?"

"Go away."

But he did not go away. Instead, he tried to sit down beside Kitty, and when one of the other passengers voiced an objection, he got a bad cussing for his trouble.

"That ties it," Kitty decided aloud as she reached into her purse and pulled out a derringer. It was a two-shot .45 with a pearl handle. Kitty had never killed a man with it, but she had scared a few nearly to death.

"You have worn out your welcome, buster! Get out of here now."

The conductor appeared. "What is the trouble?"

"This man is being belligerent," Kitty answered. "He won't leave us alone and he has a foul mouth."

"Young fella, find an empty seat and behave yourself. We have rules regarding conduct on the Atchison, Topeka and the Santa Fe and they must be obeyed."

"Oh yeah!"

"Yes," the conductor said firmly. "Now please do as I ask."

"Or you are going to throw me off, right?"

"I'm afraid you will be asked to disembark at the very next station. But that—"

To Kitty's amazement, the young ruffian grabbed the old conductor, shoved him backward down the aisle, and screamed, "I'm going to watch you 'disembark' right now, you mouthy old geezer!"

Kitty jumped up from her seat as the conductor was propelled up the aisle. "Are you crazy! Stop!"

But the troublemaker was insane with rage and intent on tossing the conductor off the train. Kitty caught a glimpse of the old man's frightened face as she ran forward shouting, "Let go of him!"

The bully wasn't listening, and when he yanked open the front door of their car, Kitty had no choice but to aim for his leg and fire the derringer.

The troublemaker screamed, twisting around and attempting to tear a gun from under his belt. He was almost within arm's reach and Kitty hesitated, not wanting to shoot to kill. The man was bleeding profusely and his eyes were crazed with either pain or hate. When his gun came out, Kitty shot him in the chest and he went down kicking and screaming.

"Oh, my heavens!" the conductor shouted. "Is anyone here a doctor!"

No one answered, so the conductor disappeared in search of help. Kitty dropped to the man's side with every intention of trying to save his life, but one look told her it was already too late.

"He's dead," Kitty said to no one in particular.

"He was crazy," the man who had tried to befriend her answered. "Drunk and crazy."

Kitty was about to reply when the door burst open, with the excited conductor waving and yelling, "Right this way, Doctor!"

The doctor knelt beside the body. He took the man's pulse and then ruefully shook his head. "I couldn't have saved him even if I'd been close. This man was shot right through the heart."

"I'm the one that shot him," Kitty said. "First in the leg, then, when he tried to kill me, I had no choice but to aim for his chest."

"Well, lady, you put this young man in his grave." The doctor looked as if he wanted to say more, but then thought better of it when Festus burst into the coach. "Marshal, I guess this is where you step in."

"Kitty!"

"Hello, Festus," she said lamely.

"What are *you* doin' on this train?"

"It's complicated," Kitty hedged. "Why don't you take care of this business and we can talk later."

Festus had the body removed and the conductor immediately had a porter clean up the bloodstains. Not much was said by anyone and Kitty felt depressed.

"There was no reason for him dying like that," she replied when Festus again pressed her for an explanation. "The man had been drinking and I probably should have just left this coach and found another empty seat."

"You still haven't told me why you left Dodge City."

"I . . . I'm going to see an old friend that lives in Grover, Colorado."

"That's where the new deputy that is fillin' in for me comes from."

"It's a small world."

"Yeah, but Kitty, you never said nothing about an old friend living out there among them homesteaders."

"Well, I don't tell you or anyone else every small detail of my past."

Her reply caught Festus off guard and he stammered, "Miss Kitty, I could—"

"No," she interrupted. "I don't think that would be a good idea. My friend is not interested in seeing anyone but me. Do you understand?"

"I'm afraid I do," he said quietly. "What did you tell Matthew about this old boyfriend?"

"Could we talk about something else? I've just been forced to kill a drunk and now you're wanting to know things about someone that I prefer not to have you or anyone else in Dodge City even know exists."

"All right."

Kitty could see that Festus was very upset and disappointed and she would have given anything to tell him the truth. However, he needed to go on to find Miss Austin, and Kitty knew he would not do this if he learned the real purpose of her visit to Grover.

When the train finally arrived at her destination, Kitty looked out the window at even more isolated scenery than she had expected. There was only a general store with three cow ponies tied in front, a corral and hay barn along with some scrubby trees fed by a whirling windmill. The nearest homestead cabin was about five miles north and all the others were mere specks on the horizon.

"Where is this 'friend'?" Festus asked as she hoisted her valise and prepared to leave the train.

"He's probably waiting in the general store."

"If he was a gentleman, he'd be waiting right here for you," Festus complained. "Miss Kitty, are you—"

"Good-bye and good luck in Colorado," she said, giving her friend a quick hug and then making her exit.

Without a backward glance, Kitty marched into the general store, where three cowboys were bellied up to a plank that served as a bar. At the sight of her, all conversation died.

An older man behind the bar wiped his hands on a dirty apron and came around to greet Kitty, saying, "Miss, this really isn't the kind of a place for you to be comin' in alone. Why don't you get back on the train now?"

"I'm looking for a man named Jack Casey."

"Casey lives about twenty miles to the northeast," the owner said. "He comes in once a week for whiskey and supplies. He won't return until next Tuesday or Wednesday."

"My name is Miss Kitty Russell," she said, addressing everyone. "I own the Long Branch Saloon in Dodge City."

"I thought I recognized you!" a thin cowboy exclaimed, showing his buckteeth. "Miss Kitty, I been in your saloon many a night drinkin' and dancin' with your girls. How is Miss Irma?"

"She's fine."

"I been in your saloon, too," his companion added. "My name is Zeke, you just spoke with Slim, and the feller at the end of the bar is Earl."

"I'm pleased to meet you," Kitty told them. "But I have

come to meet Jack Casey and I'll be needing a way out to his homestead."

"Whatever do you want to see old Jack for?" the bartender and, no doubt, owner asked. "He's kinda rough around the edges and, since his wife died a while back, not much for being social. Fact is, he's real unsociable."

"What did his wife die of?"

"Old age and consumption."

"How old is Mr. Casey?"

"Older than the hills," one of the cowboys answered. "Jack is trying to sell out but wants two hundred dollars, which is about a hundred and fifty too much . . . even considerin' his place comes with two good mules, several pigs, and a milk cow!"

They all laughed, thinking this was a great joke. But Kitty wasn't laughing. It was beginning to sound as if she had wasted her time coming all the way out here thinking that Casey would be able to help Matt.

"I need to see him today," she said, "and I'll pay for someone to drive me out there."

"My wagon is broke," the bartender said. "There might be someone bringing one in for supplies, but that's not something you could count on."

"Then I'd like to rent a horse."

"We need our horses, and anyway," Slim said with a grin, "you sure ain't dressed for riding."

"I've got a change of clothes in my valise and I'm a good horseback rider. Which one of you wants to rent me your horse?"

"How much you willin' to pay to put a cowboy afoot?" Earl asked.

"I only need the horse overnight," Kitty explained. "And I'll pay you ten dollars."

"For one night?" Zeke asked. "Ma'am, my bay gelding would be perfect."

"No," Earl argued. "The roan is smoother-gaited and just right for a lady!"

"Now wait just a darned minute here," Slim protested. "My buckskin is twice the horse that either one of them others is. Why, Old Dusty will have you out to Jack's place quicker than I can work up a good spit!"

"Yeah, but he's ornery and he most always bucks!" Earl added.

Kitty went outside. The train was almost finished re-filling its boiler as she inspected the three animals. The roan was her first choice and she paid Earl ten dollars, saying, "I'm going behind those trees to change into a riding habit and I want you to keep everyone away, then get me headed in the right direction."

"Yes, ma'am," Earl promised, looking extremely pleased with the money. "While you're changin', I'll shorten the length of my stirrups. You're going to like this horse so much you might want to buy him."

"I don't think so," Kitty replied. When she returned, all of them were standing around the roan and trying to give her directions at the same time.

"Wait a minute," she said. "Slim, why don't you tell me how to find Jack Casey."

"Well, ma'am, he lives about twenty miles yonder."

Kitty followed his pointed finger. "Are there any dirt tracks that I can follow?"

"Yes, ma'am!" Slim, with a little elaboration from his friends and the store owner, gave her detailed directions.

"Miss," the owner said, "Jack is kinda crotchety. I don't think he'd harm you, but—"

"I'm armed and plenty able to take care of myself," she informed them. "As a matter of fact, I just had to kill a man before I got off the train."

As if on cue, the conductor emerged, leading two porters carrying the shrouded body.

"Holy smokes!" the bartender whispered. "You killed that man?"

"I had no choice," Kitty answered.

"What did he do?"

"Insulted me."

"Holy cow!" Slim exclaimed. "And so you plugged him?"

"I did."

The four men exchanged glances and then Kitty saw Festus start to climb down from the train. Before he could join her and start asking more questions, she climbed onto the roan, waved good-bye, and went galloping off to find Jack Casey.

When she glanced back over her shoulder, Festus was back on the train and it was already starting to roll toward Pueblo.

Now, she thought, *this man Casey had damn sure better be worth all this grief and bother.*

CHAPTER

18

From the appearance of his ramshackle house, falling-over fences, and miserable little barn, Kitty quickly decided that Jack Casey was a poor homesteader. She did not see the milk cow or the mules, but she did observe a handsome dapple-gray horse tied to the same tree that a sleeping man was leaning against. He had a rifle cradled across his lap and his head was tipped forward.

"Hello!" she called. "Are you Mr. Jack Casey?"

The head tipped back and the rifle came up fast, pointed in her direction. Kitty could tell at once that this man was young and quick.

"Who are you and what do you want!"

"My name is Kitty Russell and I've come to talk to Mr. Casey. Doesn't he live here?"

"Yeah, I expect so."

"Would you please put that rifle down?"

"I guess."

Kitty rode up to the man, whose appearance was strikingly handsome. He had high cheekbones, perfect white

146

teeth, dark features, and was of average size. Unlike the cowboys, he wore buckskin breeches and a loose cotton shirt not tucked into his pants but belted by a cartridge belt. There was a knife in a fringed sheath hanging by a thong draped over one shoulder and a six-gun strapped on his lean hip. She had seen enough men on this wild frontier to guess that he was probably a half-breed, although his black hair was cut short and he wore a cowboy's wide-brimmed hat.

"Is Mr. Casey in the house?"

"Nope."

Kitty looked to the barn.

"Not there, either."

"All right," she said, feeling an edge of impatience, "then where is he?"

"Buried."

"Oh, damn," Kitty swore under her breath.

"What did you say, ma'am?"

"Never mind. What is your name?"

"Lone Wolf Who Sleeps by the River Which Travels Swiftly to the Sun . . . but you can just call me Wolf. I'm half-Comanche and half–U.S. Army sergeant. They say my father was Irish, but it don't matter none to me 'cause my mama's people scalped him."

"I'm Kitty Russell from Dodge City. What happened here?"

"I found two dead men laying in the yard. The old one had been shot with a big-caliber rifle—ambushed, I'd guess."

Wolf pointed to a low hill. "It was a long shot from a buffalo rifle up yonder. The younger fella must have come in to finish his man off. It was a big mistake because the old one was dying, but still alive. He shot the younger man right between the eyes. Two others up on the hill sat and waited until the old fella bled to death, then they come down and helped themselves to whatever food was inside and also a couple of mules and a milk cow."

"You could tell all that?"

"Sure. Injun read tracks heap good!" Wolf replied with a sardonic grin. "Or didn't you know that?"

Kitty ignored the question. "How long ago did this happen?"

"Yesterday, and I found them this morning."

"What happened to the bodies?"

"I buried 'em both. If that tough old man was a friend, you could dig him up, because he isn't resting very deep. I don't like picks and shovels."

"He can rest in peace, Wolf." Kitty dismounted. "I wanted to ask Jack Casey if he'd take a part-time job as a deputy in Dodge City."

"Well, I never knew him, but he was up to the job and this homesteading sure wasn't his calling."

"What are you going to do now?"

"I shot an antelope and still got some meat. I was going in the house to cook it up. Leave in the morning to track the men."

"Why?"

"Since I buried the old man for free, I figure I got a claim on them two mules and the milk cow."

"That's the way that you look at this?"

"Sure. Why should the ones who killed him get to keep 'em?"

"No reason," Kitty said.

"If the old man had kinfolks, they could have the mules and the milk cow."

"I don't think he had any living relatives. Jack Casey's wife died."

"Yeah, I found a grave and planted him next to it."

Kitty frowned. "Why didn't you go after the other two right away?"

"No hurry," Wolf replied. "Milk cows don't travel fast."

"You might need help when you catch up with the killers."

"I can handle it alone."

148

"You're that sure?"

"Yeah. You any good at cooking meat?"

"No."

Kitty led her horse over to the house and went inside. It had been ransacked. Not a single piece of furniture hadn't been smashed.

"The two men are headed east toward Dodge," Wolf said from the doorway.

"Maybe I'll ride out with you after them tomorrow," Kitty told him.

"Nope. I'd rather do it alone."

Kitty reached down and picked up several pieces of a table that had been smashed to splinters. "I'll start the stove. You get water and the meat."

"There's some corn in the barn could be boiled to eat."

Kitty was famished. "Okay. We'll have antelope and corn."

She started the fire and got water boiling for the corn. The half-breed cut thick slices of meat and Kitty found a frying pan, a couple of dishes, and one tin cup.

"Wolf, this is going to be humble."

"Better'n eatin' grass," he replied with a straight face, so that Kitty did not know if this was a Comanche joke.

That evening after dinner, they sat out from the house on the prairie and watched the stars for a while. Wolf wasn't much of a talker, but his presence was comforting and Kitty realized that she had no fear whatever of this complete stranger.

"I'll be gone when you wake up in the morning," Wolf told her when the hour grew late. "I'll maybe see you in Dodge City someday."

"I'm going with you," Kitty said. "My train won't be going back to Dodge for two more days and I can't stay at the general store."

"Then stay here and wait for the train."

"I'd rather help you catch the killers and see that they pay for their crime." Kitty sighed. "Like I told you before, I didn't even know Jack Casey, but being here at his place, visiting his wife's grave a while ago, and seeing what these men did to his home makes me mad."

"You're a woman."

"White women can kill, too."

"You have no weapons."

"I have a derringer and you have weapons I could use."

"No."

"Listen," Kitty said, "I am a good shot with either a gun or a rifle."

"This is different than shooting at cans or a stick."

"Wolf, I had to kill a man on the train just this morning."

Wolf turned to study her in the moonlight. "*You* killed a man today?"

"It's not something I'm proud of," Kitty answered, "but yes, I did. And tomorrow morning, I am riding with you after Jack Casey's killers."

Wolf studied her for a long moment, but Kitty met his eyes without looking away. Finally, he said, "Follow me, if you can keep up."

"I can keep up."

"We leave before dawn. You won't complain and make trouble?"

"No."

"Okay, then," he said, getting up and going back to the tree where she'd first seen him.

Kitty went into the house, found a blanket, and fell asleep almost instantly.

True to his word, Wolf awakened her well before dawn. The roan was already saddled and waiting outside. Without saying a word, he put his dapple into an easy lope and Kitty did the same. The borrowed roan was eager to run and she knew horses well enough to know the animal was fast. Earl was going to be furious but he could look her up in Dodge City and get his horse back along with a generous payment for his trouble.

About mid-morning, they crossed the tracks of the two horsemen, the mules, and the milk cow.

"They are traveling very slow because of the cow," Wolf informed her as he dismounted and toed a fresh cow plop. "We will overtake them early tonight."

"And then what?"

"I will give them the same chance they gave Jack Casey . . . but I refuse to dig their graves."

"We should try to arrest and deliver them to the authorities, who will try them for murder."

Wolf remounted, and when he twisted around in his saddle, he said, "You told me you would not be trouble."

"I won't be. I'll let you keep the livestock. Just help me capture and deliver the killers to a westbound train. After that, you can ride off and I'll do the rest."

"I keep everything?"

"That's right. You have my word on it."

"Okay," Wolf agreed.

"And please slow down. I'm not used to such hard riding."

"Woman from Dodge City, you *are* trouble!"

Kitty was already growing saddle sores and she was in no mood to be badgered. "You're no picnic yourself, Lobo Wolf Who Runs Right into the Sun."

Wolf shouted something over his shoulder that Kitty thought might be a Comanche cussword. But she didn't care if this wild half-breed son of a Comanche and an Irish sergeant was upset or that she'd just corrupted the proud translation of his Indian name. Things had really gone bad since she'd left Kansas and they were just about to get a whole lot worse.

CHAPTER

19

Kitty was in great pain from the saddle sores by the time the sunset finally turned the sky crimson and gold. She was far too exhausted either to appreciate the beauty or to worry that a storm was advancing from the north, creating immense thunderheads filled with fury.

"Can't we *please* slow down just a little?" she asked when Wolf stopped to examine the tracks. "Even I can see that we've almost overtaken Jack's killers."

Wolf remounted and stared ahead with such concentration that Kitty was quite sure he was not the least bit aware of her extreme discomfort.

"If they had any idea they were being followed," Wolf said, more to himself than to her, "we would have to circle around and attack them from the north. But since they don't—"

"We can rest awhile and overtake them after they have fallen asleep," Kitty told him. "That way we will be able to capture them alive."

"Why?"

"Because they'll be asleep!"

"I meant why not kill them and save all the trouble?"

"Because that is not the way it should be done. Matt Dillon would try to arrest them."

"Who is this Dillon?"

"He's the marshal of Dodge City."

"Oh, then he has sworn to commit such foolishness," Wolf replied, clearly unimpressed.

"It's not foolishness."

"It is, because we know they are guilty of killing one old man and stealing everything he owned. And being cowards, they also let him die slow. They probably even taunted him while he bled to death."

"We don't know that."

"I understand these kinds of men," Wolf said. "They would taunt him."

Kitty saw the futility of argument. She dismounted and bit back a cry of pain, because the insides of her legs were raw and burning. "Wolf, we made a deal. You can keep everything, but you must at least try to capture the men alive and deliver them to the railroad."

"So you can take them to Matt Dillon?"

"Yes."

The half-breed actually smiled when he said, "But this is Colorado. Your Marshal Dillon is in Kansas."

"I know, but—"

"If we are to do this the white man's way, according to his law, then I think these two men must be tried in Colorado, where Jack Casey's murder took place."

"If we get them to Dodge City, Matt will take care of that."

"This man means that much to you?"

"Yes," Kitty said after a moment. "And I want to do this right."

"Okay," Wolf said. "But if they kill us because we do not kill them first, then it is your fault."

"If they kill us, I will take the blame," Kitty said,

able to smile despite the pain radiating from her saddle sores.

"We rest, then," he decided. "These men are very close. Also, I'll give you something for those sore places."

"And I suppose that would be something like Comanche bear grease?"

"No, horse liniment mixed with prairie-dog fat. Good Indian medicine."

"I didn't realize Indians got saddle sores."

"They do," Wolf said, "and also other sores I will not talk about."

Kitty, realizing that she had just received a well-deserved comeuppance, said, "I apologize."

Wolf gave her his sidearm. "Are you sure that you can shoot this thing?"

"Yes."

"Show me."

"But won't they hear the gunfire?"

"No. They will think it big thunder. Listen."

Wolf was right. Kitty had been so preoccupied with her pain that she had not been listening to the boom of approaching thunder.

"We're in for a bad one, aren't we?"

Wolf nodded. "We had better find good cover as soon as we capture those men."

She looked around. There was nothing but rolling, grassy hills as far as the eye could see. "Where?"

"Maybe we will find a homestead or just a hole." Wolf shrugged his shoulders. "I don't know. Remember, I am only *half*-Comanche. Now shoot the gun."

"At what?"

"That rock," he said, pointing to one that was larger than its neighbors. "But wait until the next big thunder."

Kitty raised the pistol, took aim, and fired a moment after a particularly large and jagged bolt of lightning struck only a few miles to the north. To her amazement, the rock shattered.

"How about that!" she proudly exclaimed.

"Wrong rock," he said, straight-faced. "I wanted you to hit the *little* one."

Kitty shook her head. "If I can hit that big rock at this distance, you know I can hit a man. Let's not waste any more ammunition. Just give me the liniment and hang on to the horses while I go off a little ways and doctor myself. Okay?"

"Okay, 'Little Sure Shot' Annie Oakley."

Kitty had to laugh. "Where did you hear of her?"

"I get around," was all Wolf would say.

They waited about half an hour, with the wind rising and bolts of lightning beginning to make hot white webs across the northern sky. Kitty used that time to medicate herself; she wished she had a few shots of fortifying whiskey to go along with Wolf's stinking liniment. The half-breed stood beside the horses in the cold wind until the sun was completely down.

"It is time," Wolf said when the first cold drops of rain began pelting their faces.

Their horses were fractious and wanted to run from the onrushing storm; it was a struggle just to keep them pointed in the right direction. Kitty knew that the squall was about to hit and that it would be fierce, but perhaps short-lived, as storms often were in this hot season. She also knew that the tracks they followed would quickly be washed away. Maybe that was why Wolf had been pushing so hard.

"Stay close behind!" he yelled into the tearing sky, filled with thunder and lightning. "We are almost upon them!"

Kitty didn't realize how close they were until they galloped over a rise and a fork of lightning lit up the prairie for just long enough to see the killers and their stolen livestock huddled in a draw. Kitty had the impression that Casey's murderers were on foot, trying to control their stock, but she could not be certain. Even less certain was the way in which Wolf intended to confront them.

"Let's arrest them!" he shouted, voice barely audible over the storm.

"What . . . "

Wolf charged down the slope, a figure seen only in searing white snatches. Kitty sent her roan down the slope after the half-breed, without any idea of what was about to happen. She thought she heard Wolf shouting and she imagined she heard a scattering of gunfire. And suddenly she was slamming into the milk cow and the mules were running off and braying and everything was chaos. Winks of gunfire played across the inky darkness like playful fireflies; she tried to identify a target, but was afraid of shooting Wolf by mistake.

"Wolf!"

Her roan staggered and Kitty instinctively hauled up on the reins, trying to help the animal. But the roan kept falling and then Kitty felt the stunning force of the earth and nothing more.

She awoke with a headache so intense that she was certain she'd broken her skull or it had been pierced by a bullet. For several moments she lay very still, eyes unfocused but dazzled by the glistening rain-drenched grass. The earth seemed to undulate, and when she glanced up at the sky, the warm sun had an exact twin.

"Wolf," she whispered, forcing herself to sit but causing the world to swirl.

Kitty saw everything in twos. Only by squinting could she tell the horses were unsaddled and hobbled, grazing contentedly except for Earl's borrowed roan, which was dead. The milk cow was staring suspiciously at her and the mules were roped together at their tails; only the half-breed and his dapple gelding were gone.

"Wolf!"

Kitty's ears were ringing and her throat felt as if she'd

swallowed sand. Her stomach lurched and she vomited, then fell back again on the horse blanket where she'd been sleeping. Cold sweat erupted from every pore on her body and she closed her eyes, wanting more sleep.

"Miss," Wolf whispered, "you need to see a doctor and then rest."

Kitty opened her eyes to see two of him kneeling beside her. Behind him stood the dapple, head down, munching on grass. "What happened?"

"You had a bad fall. There was blood in your ears, so, if you can't hear me—"

"I can hear you. What happened to them?"

"They decided to fight. Should I leave 'em for the birds or sling 'em across the backs of their horses before we start for Dodge City?"

"You shot them?"

"Yeah, sure."

Kitty moaned. "I . . . I can't think clearly. Everything I see is hazy and double."

"Then I guess I'll leave the bodies."

"No!" Her sudden reaction caused another spear to embed itself in her throbbing skull. "Wolf, we have to take them in."

"Why? Never mind. Okay."

"Thanks."

"Can you ride?"

"What if I said no?"

His eyes crinkled at the corners and she thought he laughed. It was a rusty sound and it came to her that he did not laugh often.

"Then I would have to drape you across the saddle like those other two. The blood would all rush to your head and it might feel better, but probably a lot worse."

"That would be impossible." She felt tears in her eyes. "Wolf, do you think I can make it?"

"You have to," he said quietly. "Maybe we will go to

the Arkansas and I will make you a travois. It would be easier."

"That's one of those . . . those Indian things you drag, isn't it?"

"Yes."

"I would like that. It hurts so much to sit up."

"You have to for a while, until we return to the river."

Kitty said nothing. A few minutes later he was washing her battered face with water from his canteen.

"You're a good man, Wolf. You could have just left me."

"I thought about it."

"I'm glad you decided not to."

"Me, too," he told her as he plugged his canteen and went to gather the animals.

Somehow, he got her onto one of the dead men's horses and they started off. Wolf stayed close, knee to knee as they rode south toward the distant river. And later he made a travois as promised.

"This is living," she said, trying to sound brave.

"It will be rough," he replied. "Maybe you will want to ride on the horse again before long."

Kitty gripped the bark of the cottonwood poles and said, "Tie me down and get me to Dodge."

"Is there a good doctor there?"

"Yes."

"And your Marshal Dillon."

"Yes, he will be there, too."

"Will there be trouble over the bad men's horses, the old man's mules, and milk cow?"

"I will buy them for you myself if there is a problem."

"What about the two men I just killed?"

"If I live, I will tell Matt all that you have done for me and how you buried Jack Casey. Perhaps Matt will even ask you to be his deputy for a while."

"That would be a mistake."

"Would it?"

"Yes. And besides, I would probably say no," Wolf replied as he mounted his horse and grabbed the lead rope to the animal that would pull her into Dodge City.

"Matt Dillon can be very persuasive."

"No matter, because I can be very stubborn."

Kitty lost track of the days that followed. She was sick and dizzy and must have looked terrible when Wolf finally dragged what was left of her into Dodge City. To say that their arrival caused a sensation would be a vast understatement, according those who described the event a few weeks later when her vision was clear again and her head no longer felt as if it were about to explode.

"How did you get Wolf to agree to be your deputy?" she asked Matt one evening as he sat beside her bed while they played checkers.

"I told him that I needed a man that I could trust."

"And that's all?"

Matt smiled. "And I told him that if he helped me out until we learn if Festus is coming back, then I'd buy him a wagon and see that he gets a freight contract to go along with those mules and horses."

"Hmm," Kitty mused. "I didn't think money mattered to Wolf."

"It mattered." Matt frowned. "Do you think Wolf ever gave those men a chance to surrender?"

"I don't know," Kitty said truthfully. "But he brought me back alive and he didn't leave their bodies for the birds."

"He would have done that?"

"What choice would he have had without a shovel?"

Matt nodded in agreement then said what was really on his mind. "I just don't want someone under me that shoots first and asks questions later."

"Wolf is a good man," Kitty said. "If you ask rather than tell him how you want things done, he will be all right."

"Yeah," Matt said. "When he brought you and those two dead men into town, he sure made an impression. The worst sorts in town are giving him plenty of respect."

"Lobo Wolf Who Runs Right into the Sun deserves our respect."

"Is that *really* his full Comanche name?" Matt asked with surprise.

"No," Kitty answered, "but it's just close enough to make that man smile."

CHAPTER

20

"Marshal, are you dead sure you never heard of Doug Austin?" Festus asked one more time.

"Nope," the marshal of Goldpan snapped impatiently. "But like I told you yesterday and the day before yesterday, there are a lot of men comin' and goin' in my town and I danged sure don't know all their names."

"But you do remember Miss Clara?"

"Of course! We don't often get a *lady* come visit this raw mining town. Wish we did. Lots of men here could stand to see that kind once in a while instead of the low kind of women that come for a miner's gold."

"Thanks," Festus said, heading for the door.

"You'd better start checking on some of the other boomtowns, Marshal Haggen."

Festus halted, hand on the doorknob. "Like I told you once before, I ain't a marshal no more."

"Try Silver Gulch," the man suggested. "There's a big strike going on over there. Maybe that's where that man and his woman headed."

"She *ain't* his woman! I told you she was his sister."

"Whatever you say!" The marshal began to laugh and Festus slammed the door on him.

Discouraged and confused, Festus tried to figure out his next move as he idly surveyed this hell-on-wheels boomtown. Goldpan was already in swift decline. People were hurrying off to stake their claims at Silver Gulch or a half-dozen other new strikes. They were tearing shacks, stores, and tents down on the run and hauling Goldpan away one brick and board at a time.

The *Goldpan Gazette* was located just across the street and he saw the editor standing in the open doorway looking glum. No doubt he was watching the decline of his already slim readership. It occurred to Festus that the newspaperman might have heard of Doug Austin or been paid a visit by Clara.

The muddy main street was filled with traffic, so Festus had to wait several minutes before he could get across and speak to the editor.

"No," the man said, "however, I have heard of a *Ted* Austin. But I don't suppose—"

"Now, hold on jest a minute," Festus said quickly. "Maybe I *am* looking for a Ted Austin or he's Doug's relative. Is he still around?"

"Not likely. He was chased out of town about a month back. The crowd almost lynched him."

Festus blinked. "Why?"

"He was a crooked and not very skilled gambler who made a lot of money dealing from a badly marked deck."

"Then I doubt if he's the one that I was looking for," Festus said. "And the truth be known, I really am looking for his sister, Clara."

"Don't you mean *Sarah*?"

"No, Clara."

"Hmm, that's funny."

"What is funny?"

"I met a Sarah Austin and she was looking for a Ted Austin."

Festus made a face. "Mister, I'm getting more confused by the minute. Let me describe Miss Clara. She is about—oh, five foot three inches tall, with reddish-blond hair and kinda greenish-brown eyes. Real pretty thing."

"Did she have dimples in her cheeks?"

"Why, yes!"

"That's the one that told me her name was Sarah Austin. I recall her very well. Are you related to the young lady?"

"I'd like to be." Festus nervously wrung his hands and added, "I sorta fell in love with her."

"But you don't know if the man Sarah or Clara was looking for is Ted or Doug?"

"Her name is Clara, all right. Miss Clara Austin from Austin, Texas."

"I can't tell you where she went," the editor answered. "All I do know is that one day she was in town, the next she was gone. Maybe the woman left for faraway places or she might be living in the next boomtown on this mountain."

Festus tried to hide his disappointment. "I guess I'll just have to keep looking."

"She's searching for someone named Doug or Ted, and you're looking for her. That's quite a puzzle, all right."

"I expect so."

The editor's eyes brightened. "You know what?"

"No, sir."

"It strikes me that this would make an interesting story for my paper. Would you mind giving me some more details so that I can write it up?"

"I . . . well, sir, I don't think I better do that just now."

"Why not? I'd make it a front-page feature."

"This is all kinda personal."

"You're in love with Clara or Sarah, aren't you."

It wasn't a question and Festus knew that it would be

silly to lie about the fact. "Yeah, I am. I'm fixin' to ask her to marry me."

"Sensational! If I write a love story about how you came to find her, she might read it and respond! That way, we'd be helping each other, wouldn't we?"

"Yeah, but . . . "

The editor took Festus by the arm and guided him back into his cluttered office. After muttering and rummaging around for several minutes, he finally located a notepad and pencil. "Now, let's begin at the beginning."

"I was filling in as the marshal of Dodge City when Miss Clara came up from Austin, Texas, on a stage. You see, Matt Dillon got his leg broken and . . . "

Nearly two hours later Festus walked back outside with the excited newspaperman close on his heels.

"Marshal Haggen, I'll write this story up and it will be in the Sunday edition. And while I admit that my readership is small and getting smaller every day, I can also tell you that a newspaper gets a lot of rereads and is passed from camp to camp."

"So Clara really might see this and know I'm here looking to ask for her hand in marriage."

"Of course! And if that happens, I'll have an even better story. Tell me, have you bought a wedding ring yet?"

"Well, no, sir. I ain't sure if she'll marry me even if I do find her."

"You'll find Miss Austin if she is still in the gold district," the editor promised. "Your story will be circulated far and wide. The headline on this article will be smashing and sell lots of copies."

"And what will it be?"

"Oh," the newsman mused "I'm not sure yet but something like . . . 'Dodge City Lawman Tracks Down Love.'"

"But I ain't a lawman no more."

"In answer to that, I have an old newsman's saying that I have found extremely profitable."

Festus frowned. "Which is?"

"Don't let the *de-tails* stand in the way of *de-sales*!" The man chuckled at the rhyming play on words. "See what I'm getting at?"

"Yeah, but—"

"Marshal Haggen, it has been a supreme pleasure! And I mean that most sincerely. Just hang around a couple of days and I'm sure that Miss Sarah will come running into your arms."

"I hope so."

"So do I! And if she does, you must promise to allow me the pleasure and the profit of doing a follow-up interview with both of you enraptured with wedded bliss."

"Huh?"

The editor pumped Festus's hand up and down like a handle. "Thanks, Marshal, and don't forget to bring her to my office after you get married!"

Festus was dubious about what he'd just done, but since he had no leads and not the slightest idea of where to go next looking for Clara, he really had no choice.

"I sure thank you, Mister . . . "

"Mr. Jackson. Harvey Jackson."

"All right, Mr. Jackson."

"And don't forget to buy her a wedding ring!" the editor called as he hurried off to write the story. "A woman can't refuse a real diamond, you know."

Festus thought about that for a minute and realized Mr. Jackson was right. If he proposed marriage and had no ring, Clara might think that he wasn't real serious . . . or, worse yet, that he thought her not worth spending money upon.

"I better see if I can find a wedding ring," he said to himself as he turned to look up and down the muddy street.

Fortunately, there was a jewelry store still left standing, but the owner was already starting to pack his goods away in preparation for leaving Goldpan. When Festus explained that he wanted to buy a wedding ring, the man's eyes turned warm and friendly.

"That's wonderful, Mister . . . "

"Haggen. Festus Haggen."

"And who might the lucky young lady be?"

"Miss Clara or Sarah—you see, I'm not sure anymore which—Austin."

"You can't remember her name?" The man's bushy eyebrows lifted.

"It's a long story."

"Ha! I see." The jeweler winked. "A man has a little too much to drink and meets a woman then the next thing you know—"

"That ain't it atall!"

"It is not important that I know her name," the jeweler said, smile evaporating as he escorted Festus over to a case of rings. "Pick out the one that you like and I'll make it a bargain."

"How much are they?" Festus said, staring through a glass countertop at a display of rings, most of which were adorned with diamonds.

"They range in price from two dollars to five hundred dollars. Of course, the two-dollar rings aren't genuine. The stones are glass, the metal polluted with copper, but then, how many women know the difference?"

"I wouldn't want to fool Miss Sarah. But what if she don't want to marry me?"

"You haven't even asked your intended yet?"

"No, I can't find her."

The jeweler opened his mouth to say something, then changed his mind and forced a smile. "How much money did you want to spend on Sarah or Clara?"

Festus dragged out his wallet. He had withdrawn all of his recent savings, but expenses had been higher than anticipated. Prices were terrible in the mining towns and he was down to just under four hundred dollars.

"I could spend maybe a hundred dollars," he told the eager jeweler.

"That will get you real gold and a real diamond or two, but they will not be impressive. And you are an impressive gentleman. Still, if you insist on being a skinflint . . ."

"Then what can I get for two hundred?"

"Now you're talking quality," the jeweler told him. "Take a look at this one!"

Twenty minutes and two hundred and eighty dollars later, Festus had a ring to make any woman proud. Sure, he was down to little more than a hundred dollars, but that would hold them until he could find another job. And he had a hunch that most of these towns could use a good lawman like himself. Why, just looking around, Festus could see all manner of things going on that would not have been tolerated in Dodge City.

He found a hotel that was not yet being dismantled, and settled in, determined to find day work and stop cutting into his cash reserves until he and Clara got married and decided what they wanted to do and where to live. Festus was hoping that Clara would agree to return to Dodge City, where they'd met and fallen in love. He wanted to go back to work for Matthew and it didn't matter all that much that he'd only be a lowly deputy again.

Two long and impatient days later Sunday rolled around and Festus was one of the first to buy the *Goldpan Gazette*.

But when his eyes snapped on the headline and he read, LOVESICK MARSHAL SEEKING MISS CLARA . . . OR MISS SARAH? he felt something as hard and heavy as a cannonball form in his gut. The feeling didn't get much better when he read on and realized that the editor had written the entire piece in jest, poking fun not only at Festus, but at the "elusive and mysterious bride of his fantastic dreams."

"I'm gonna strangle him like a rabbit!" Festus growled as he stormed out of his hotel room and marched up the street.

But the *Goldpan Gazette* was gone . . . the whole building! And to make matters worse, standing across the street was the town marshal and a group of his cronies pointing at Festus and laughing like a pack of hyenas!

It was enough to make a grown man cry. Festus stomped off shouting imprecations at the folks still left in this awful town, who all seemed to delight in his acute embarrassment. He would buy—no, he was running too short of money—he would rent a horse and head for Silver Gulch and see if he could find Sarah or, at the very least, that miserable Harvey Jackson to throttle.

CHAPTER

21

Silver Gulch was as busy as an anthill, with hundreds of men erecting a business section that, as far as Festus could tell, mostly consisted of saloons. The boomtown was situated down in a deep gulch, which Festus thought prime for springtime flooding and deep winter snows. All the local talk centered on the exciting new gold and silver deposits being discovered in the creeks that bled down from the surrounding mountains into this deep, shadowy gulch.

One of the first people that Festus spotted was the newspaper editor Harvey Jackson. He had two burly employees hammering boards together while he worked in a ragged tent, trying to get out the first edition of his new *Silver Gulch Grunt*.

"I found you!" Festus grated as he stepped into the tent to confront the man.

"Marshal Haggen, well, hello! What a pleasant surprise to see you again so soon. How did you get here?"

"I walked."

"Long walk."

"I'm getting used to it," Festus said, not bothering to mention that he had decided to forgo the renting of a horse after learning it would cost him two dollars a day . . . plus feed. Right now his mood was as sore as his feet.

"Did your beloved find you in Goldpan?"

"No, she didn't," he responded, "and I dang sure don't appreciate you makin' fun of Miss Clara and me, either!"

"Is it Clara . . . or Sarah?" Jackson asked, trying to make a joke.

"It's Clara and don't you try to wiggle outta the fact that you lied to me!" Festus rolled up his sleeves and advanced with clenched fists. "Put 'em up and let's settle this thing right now."

"Wait a minute here!" Jackson cried, nearly spilling out of his chair and backpedaling across his tent. "Now, Marshal, there is no need to commit violence!"

"I disagree!"

"Marshal, now just settle down or I'll have to enlist the aid of my two stout employees. You don't want to be attacked by three of us, do you?"

The pair of workmen appeared. The bigger of the two stuck his head in the tent and asked, "You need some help, Mr. Jackson?"

"I . . . I'm not sure."

The man glared at Festus, a hammer still clenched in his big fist. "If this man gives you any trouble, you call us, okay?"

"I sure will," the editor replied.

The workmen disappeared and Jackson said, "Now, let's cool down and discuss whatever has upset you."

"You know danged good and well why I'm upset. You have a mean way of poking fun at a fella trying to get hisself married to the girl he loves."

"Listen, I admit that I sort of went overboard on the humorous part, but I wrote it in the great tradition of another editorial humorist, Mark Twain. That kind of story makes people laugh—"

"At *my* expense?"

"I apologize," Jackson said. "I am sorry, but things were pretty grim in Goldpan and I was just trying to raise everyone's spirits."

"None of that matters to me."

"Tell you what . . . I'll write a *second* article that will be serious and will attract even greater—"

"Oh no, you don't," Festus warned, fists clenching again. "I was pretty near laughed out of Goldpan and I ain't gonna let that happen again. You just write and poke fun about other folks, but not any more about me and Miss Clara."

The editor sighed. "You are making me feel extremely guilty. At least allow me to write a second article, which you can read and have editorial approval over before I set it in type."

Festus squinted at the man with suspicion. "What does that mean . . . exactly?"

"It means you can change any wording you wish. And I guarantee you that if Miss Austin is anywhere within a hundred miles of Silver Gulch, she will come running."

"Naw, I don't think so."

"Have you had any success finding her here in Silver Gulch?"

"Not yet, but—"

"Well then, what do you have to lose?"

Festus hitched up his pants. He'd lost weight trudging around in these steep Rocky Mountains and his appearance wasn't dandy anymore. His new boots and suit were caked and splattered with mud. He needed a shave, a bath, and a haircut, but hated the price he'd have to pay to get them in these boomtowns.

"All right, then," Jackson said, taking Festus's silence for consent. "Another interview—serious this time, mind you—another article appealing to anyone who might know of Miss Clara Austin's whereabouts to come forth. How much fairer could I possibly be?"

"Not much, I guess." Festus looked around. "I could use some work. I bought Clara a wedding ring and I'm gettin' low on cash."

"Hmm, I suppose I could use another carpenter for a few days. How does two dollars a day sound?"

"Sounds good," Festus replied, not bothering to tell the man that sixty a month was nearly twice what he'd been making as Matthew's deputy back in Dodge City. But then, everything in Colorado was higher than a hound's backbone, so it all came out about the same.

"Can you build?"

"Sure!"

"Hammer a nail and saw straight cuts in wood?"

Festus rolled up his sleeves and flexed his muscles. "I'm strong and no stranger to hard work."

"Then let's do another interview, and then you can grab a saw and get busy."

"Suits me right down to the ground, Harvey."

"Mr. Jackson," the editor corrected. "If you're on my payroll, you have to call me Mr. Jackson."

"Fine," Festus agreed while the editor of the *Silver Gulch Grunt* rummaged around for a pencil and pad of paper.

Mr. Jackson's second article was serious instead of jocular and tongue-in-cheek like the first one. It was so appealing and well written that complete strangers stepped forward to tell Festus that they hoped he found Miss Austin and they got hitched. He even had a couple of fellas offer to play fiddles and guitars if they married in Silver Gulch.

And then, two days after the article appeared and while Festus was busily hammering on the rooftop, Miss Clara appeared.

"Holy hog fat," Festus whispered as she walked purposefully toward the newspaper building. "Miss Clara!"

It was warm and he'd removed his vest and coat to work in his undershirt. Clara glanced up and saw him all sweaty and grimy and didn't even break stride as she entered the office below.

Festus threw his hammer down and grabbed his vest and coat. He'd lost his tie and was filthy and smelled like a pig, but he knew that none of that mattered as he scrambled down the ladder and bounded into Mr. Jackson's office.

"Darlin', I found you!" he shouted, swooping Clara up in his arms and swinging her around in two complete circles.

"Festus? Festus, put me down!"

He did as she told him, smelling her hair and basking in her lovely presence.

For a moment she seemed speechless and then blurted, "What happened to you, Festus?"

"Uh . . . what do you mean?"

She cocked her head to one side. "You look terrible!"

Suddenly he was stammering and out of words. "Well Miss Clara, I—"

"Miss Austin," the editor interrupted, "tell me, is your first name Sarah . . . or Clara? There seems to be a great deal of confusion."

"It's Clara."

"See," Festus crowed, getting back in balance, "and her brother is named Doug, ain't it, Miss Clara?"

A shadow passed across her pretty face and Festus thought he saw her eyes mist with tears. "Did I say something wrong?"

"No, but this is difficult for me to talk about."

"But you must!" Jackson exclaimed. "After all, this man quit a very important job in Dodge City to find and marry you."

"I . . . I know," she replied, eyes pinned on Festus

alone. "I read the article in your paper. Festus, we have to talk right away."

"Okay, Miss Clara."

"What's to talk about!" the editor cried. "Propose marriage to her!"

He scrambled for writing materials. "But not before I am ready to catch the immortal words you are about to utter."

"Mr. Jackson, you're makin' fun of us again."

"No I'm not!"

"Yes you are," Clara snapped. "You're most certainly making fun, and we'll have none of it today! Festus, let's go for a walk, but for heaven's sakes, please stay downwind!"

"Yes, ma'am."

"It's not off to a very good beginning, is it?" Jackson asked as they were leaving.

"Shut up!" Clara cried. "This is no time for joking!"

Festus swung around, fists clenched. "Miss Clara, do you want me to rearrange the way his head sits on his narrow shoulders?"

"No, let's just leave!"

"Yes, ma'am."

"And please stop 'ma'amming' me to death!"

"Yes, Miss Clara."

They started down the street, him walking a little ways off to the side, her with those beautiful eyes locked on something straight ahead. Festus was aware that a lot of folks had stopped what they were doing and had come out to watch. A couple of fools even broke into applause when he escorted Miss Clara around a corner and out toward a big new livery barn under construction.

"Now," she said, coming to a halt, "I must have an understanding."

"I thought we did," he replied. "We love each other."

"I . . . well, I am not quite sure that is true anymore," she told him with downcast eyes.

That caused Festus to feel as if someone had poleaxed

him in the gizzard. All of a sudden he was feeling mighty weak.

"Why don't we sit down," Clara suggested, indicating a couple of nearby boxes.

"Good idea," was all Festus could manage to say as they took seats side by side, but not even touching.

"Festus, I feel badly about what has happened. Did you really buy me a wedding ring like it said in today's newspaper?"

"I sure did! It's real pretty, Miss Clara. And listen, I know I look sort of poor and smell like a dirty varmint, but—"

"That's not it," she interrupted. "I wasn't completely honest with you in Dodge City."

"You weren't?" He stopped digging into his pocket for the ring.

"No. I was afraid, and feeling very vulnerable. You appeared so dashing and brave and . . . well, I lost my senses and never recovered them in Dodge City."

He took a deep breath, realizing how it was going to go now and wanting to salvage just a thread of his dignity. "I guess that we had so much fun and things happened so fast we both got a little carried away, huh?"

"That's it exactly," she said, looking relieved. "And it wasn't until I was on the train that I realized that I'd acted stupidly and—"

"Aw, it wasn't stupid. We . . . well, we had a real special time together, didn't we?"

She reached out and took his rough hand. "We had a *magical* time together, Festus. But I never dreamed that you'd quit your job and come after me."

"I never been in love like this before. But then, maybe it wasn't really love atall," he lied. "Maybe, maybe it was like you said . . . just sort of losing our senses."

"I suppose."

Clara didn't release his hand, nor did she seem to notice how Festus required a handkerchief to blow his nose and dry his own fool eyes.

"I need your help," she told him, "though heaven knows I don't deserve it."

"You want me to find Doug, is that it?"

"His name is really Ted," she confessed. "And yes, I am desperate to find him."

"Is he really your brother, or did you also make that story up?"

"Festus, I'm sorry to have to tell you this, but Ted is my husband."

Festus took a couple deep gulps of pure Rocky Mountain air and was mighty glad that he was seated. "Then I guess we can't get married, huh?"

"No, we can't. But I really don't love the man. Not anymore. I did once, but then Ted changed. When we met in Austin, he said his name was Doug, but later I learned it was really Theodore."

"I see."

"No," she said quietly, "you don't. I was twenty years old and even more foolish with my heart than I am now. We had a daughter."

"You did?" Festus's head snapped up. "Where is she?"

"Back home in Texas, being cared for by my parents. Mary is only four years old and so I would never have thought of bringing her into this wild and lawless country."

"Why'd you even want to find a man who'd desert you and your little girl?" Festus asked, his mind now off his own broken heart and focused on a little girl who probably had her mother's sweet angel face.

"Ted has some unfinished business he has to take care of back in Austin," she answered. "Also, he never said goodbye to his daughter and she deserves an explanation."

"Why, I reckon that she does, but—"

"And there are some financial matters that he *must* help me take care of. I need Ted's signature on some very important documents. They are so important that I, as well as most of my family, will become destitute if they are not signed and recorded by my husband."

"Oh, now I am starting to understand," Festus heard himself say.

She squeezed his hand. "You are a true gentleman and I can see how much pain I've caused you and am very, very sorry."

"Aw, that's all right."

"What about your job in Dodge City? Can you get it back?"

"I guess so." Festus tried to smile. "I'm not sure that I want it back, though."

"Why not?"

"I feel like a fool. When I met you, I was kinda bustin' at the britches, you might say. But if I go back, I'll be just an old nothing deputy again and—"

"Then *don't* go back to Dodge City. Find a marshal's job right here in Silver Gulch or in some other Rocky Mountain mining town and make a new and a better life for yourself."

"I dunno if I'm up to that."

"Of course you are! You were marshal caliber in my eyes and in the eyes of everyone else in Dodge City when we were there together. You can be in Colorado as well."

"I don't feel much like anything right now." This was a huge understatement. In truth, Festus was feeling lower than dirt. "I guess I'll just keep workin' for Mr. Jackson until the work runs out and then I'll move on."

"Festus, listen to me! I hurt you badly, but I can't change that because it is done. I led you on and I am ashamed of myself. But I do have a little money, which I'll gladly give to you if you help me find my husband and make him come back to Austin to do what is right by my daughter and my family."

"What, exactly, did he do?"

"I . . . I can't tell you."

"Why not?"

"There will probably be a trial. My attorney insisted that I say nothing until Ted has to go before a judge and give his testimony. When I stand up in court before the judge, one of the questions he or my husband's attorney could ask is if I divulged some very secret and important information."

Festus pulled his hand away and stood up. He ran his fingers through his shock of unruly hair and absently picked away at blotchy red mud stains all over his once handsome suit. He felt used and worthless.

"I will pay you a hundred dollars right now."

"I don't know if I could do anything," Festus said honestly. "My mind is just sort of all jumbled up."

"May I see the wedding ring you bought for me?"

"I—"

"It must be on your person. Please, Festus!"

His hand went deep into his pants pocket and out came the little box, which he gave to Clara without opening. "It's not so much of a ring, really."

Now her eyes did spill over with tears as she stared at the ring and then tried it on. "Festus, it's the most beautiful ring in the whole world!"

He believed Clara but her words made him feel worse, not better. "I guess it even fits."

"Yes," she told him. "It does. But I'm still married."

"Yeah, but I'd like you to keep it anyway."

"I can't."

"Then give it to your little girl as a present someday," he said, starting to feel sick and wanting to walk away.

"Festus, help me! Help me find Ted and take him back to Austin. Maybe there and then we can put what we had in Dodge City back together."

"I'm not sure that I could."

"Try!"

"I'll think about it some," he told her as he quickly walked away.

CHAPTER

22

When Festus returned to his job helping to put a roof on the newspaper office, no one had much to say to him because it was obvious that something had gone amiss. Festus hammered nails, sawed boards, and worked like a crazy man, and the other two employees stayed out of his way.

"Festus," the newspaperman called as the sun began to slide behind the western peaks, "it's quitting time."

"I'll be finishing up soon, Mr. Jackson."

The newspaper editor frowned, then returned to his desk and worked another hour by lamplight. When it became fully dark and Festus had not climbed down from the roof, Jackson went back outside and saw him squatting on his haunches with his head bent and cradled in his hands.

Though somewhat afraid of heights, Jackson climbed up the ladder to sit beside the ex-lawman from Dodge City. "I take it things went very badly, huh?"

"Yeah," Festus replied, raising his head and gazing morosely at the stars. "Turns out Clara is married and looking for her husband here in these gold camps."

The editor heaved a deep sigh, then said, "I'm very sorry to hear that. I think most every man in this camp has enough of a romantic streak to have hoped it would work out between you and *Mrs*. Austin."

"Well, it won't."

"Then you'll be returning the wedding ring?"

"Nope. I gave it to her anyway."

There was another long pause, then Jackson asked, "You *gave* Mrs. Austin the diamond ring, even though she is already married?"

"Sure. After all, it fit her a whole lot better than me."

The attempt at humor failed miserably and neither of them laughed. Festus added, "I didn't want it back and Clara has a daughter that she could give it to."

"My heavens, man, that was a very expensive ring!"

"She says she doesn't love her husband anymore and that he deserted her back in Texas. Clara wants me to help her find Ted Austin and bring him back home to stand before a judge for some things he's done wrong."

"Ah! Then she wants a divorce!" Jackson tried to sound enthusiastic. "That's good news, isn't it? You and she can be wed after this messy affair is settled in court."

"Maybe." Festus took a deep breath. "She offered me a hundred dollars to help her find her husband. I told her that I'd think about it."

"What's there to 'think about'?"

"I dunno," Festus answered. "I'm just not sure how I feel about Clara anymore. She fed me a bunch of lies in Dodge City and I don't much care for that."

"The poor woman was desperate! Abandoned by a cad and left in the lurch! Surely you must sympathize with her plight. She probably fell head over heels in love with you and then felt terrible. So terrible that she couldn't bring herself to confess the truth. Come on, Festus, have a little empathy and understanding!"

"I'm trying my best to, Mr. Jackson. But it might take a while."

"You don't have the luxury of time," Jackson snapped. "If the woman is willing to pay to have someone help her find her wayward husband, then she will have no shortage of takers. If you want my advice—"

"Which I don't."

"Which you will receive anyway," Jackson pushed on, "you'll help the young woman find her husband and escort him back to Texas in handcuffs and shackles! Then, being the hero that you are, a divorce will be granted quickly and you can be wed."

"I dunno."

Jackson frowned with perplexity. "Is it the idea of having a daughter that you didn't father that you find so objectionable?"

"I hadn't even thought at it, but, no, I always wanted kids to help raise. Clara said the girl was just four years old and I'm sure she could use a better father."

"Well, then?"

Festus ran his fingers through his unwashed and tangled hair. "I think I'm going to quit on you, Mr. Jackson. Tonight I'm going to have me a bottle of whiskey and then tomorrow a bath, haircut, and shave. After that, I'll decide if I want to go back to Dodge or help Clara find that . . . that scoundrel."

"I hope you decide to help her. The pay is good and it would do wonders for your heart. I'm going back down now and have myself a couple of toots. How about joining me? Neither of us can get drunk up here and it wouldn't be a healthy idea even if we could."

Festus smiled. "You're not such a bad man as I thought after that first article, Mr. Jackson. In fact, I—"

"Now, now!" Jackson slapped him on the shoulder. "Festus, let's get tight!"

"Suits me right down to the ground, Mr. Jackson."

"When you drink with me, we are equals. Besides, you just quit your job, didn't you?"

"Yes, sir."

"Then you may simply call me Harvey."

That night, Festus and Harvey made the rounds of the saloons, most of which were just tents and some that were nothing more than a couple of planks stretched between whiskey and beer barrels. Festus was in no mood for condolences from the other patrons and Harvey kept them at bay, which was greatly appreciated. Festus also noted that the editor drank with one hand and took notes for his future columns with the other.

In the morning, Festus paid heavily for his bath, shave, and haircut. He had his boots shined and his suit cleaned and pressed. His once creamy-white Stetson was nearly beyond redemption, but the barber powdered it so heavily it looked nearly new when Festus started for the street.

"Just don't get caught wearing that Stetson in the rain and it'll keep lookin' good," was the barber's sage advice. "Otherwise, that talc powder will run and it'll look pretty awful."

"I'll try to keep outta the rain," Festus promised as he headed for a nearby café, determined to have a good big breakfast and linger over coffee until he'd made what he expected was one of the most fateful decisions of his entire life.

"Morning, Marshal," the owner of the café said in respectful greeting. "Sure sorry things didn't work out between you and that pretty lady."

"Thanks." The last thing that Festus needed or wanted was sympathy. "I'll have ham and eggs. Lots of them both, with coffee."

"Comin' right up!"

The coffee was hot and strong, and since he had not drunk too much whiskey the night before, Festus was feeling better. He decided it would probably be best if he returned to Dodge City and asked Matthew for his job. If that wasn't possible, he would move on and maybe find another marshal to work for, although the thought of doing so was not very appealing. He and Matthew were a team, and there wasn't anyone else that Festus could imagine working with as harmoniously. Still, he had to work. He'd spent most all of his savings and a man had to eat.

"Here you go, Marshal," the owner said, "you put this plate of ham, eggs, and toast under your belt and things will soon look a whole lot brighter."

"Thanks," Festus said, aware that everyone in the café was watching him closely. What did they suppose? That he was going to run a knife across his throat or break down and bawl like a baby?

Festus pushed those thoughts aside and attacked his breakfast. He'd made his decision and he would be leaving Silver Gulch today . . . on foot. He'd have to pass through Goldpan on his way down the mountain, but he could sort of swing around what was left of that dying town and then trudge the rest of the way on down to Pueblo. He had enough money to buy a return train ticket and he could be in Dodge City in four or five days, if everything went right. After that, it was up to Matt Dillon what he'd be doing next.

"Festus?"

The café went silent and Festus glanced up to see Clara standing by his table in a pink dress so pretty it made his heart ache.

"Festus, can I please join you for breakfast?"

"Sure," he said, not sure at all if he wanted to be near her again. It would make leaving only harder.

"Ma'am, can I take your order?"

"I'll have about a third of what Festus has on his plate, please."

"Yes, ma'am!"

"And tea instead of coffee."

"Comin' right up!"

Festus had suddenly lost his appetite, but he'd paid for

the meal, which was going to be expensive, and he figured he had better eat well if he was going to walk all the way back to Pueblo.

"Festus, you look very nice this morning."

"Thanks," he replied, trying to avoid looking at her too much.

"Have you decided to help me find Ted?"

He laid his knife and fork down and took a slurp of coffee before trusting himself to answer. "I reckon I'm heading back to Dodge City to try and get back my deputy job."

She blinked rapidly, then whispered, "Oh."

"Clara, I'm sorry. But for a hundred dollars, you can hire plenty of men to help you find Mr. Austin."

"I can, but not very many would be willing . . . or capable of protecting my life."

Festus gulped. " 'Protecting your life'?"

"Yes, Ted will resist coming back to Texas."

"Why?"

"Because he'll go to jail for some of the things he did in Austin." Clara leaned forward. "Festus, you protected me the very first time we met. Please don't let me down now. If something should happen to me, what would become of my baby girl!"

Before he could think of a reply, there were those tears welling up in her pretty eyes again. Festus's resolve to put Clara behind him went right out the window. "You never said nothin' about him being violent."

"He is *very* violent."

"And he'd hurt, or even kill you?"

"Yes, he would. You don't know Ted."

"And I don't want to know him."

Desperation tore at the edges of her voice. "Festus, there is no one else that I can trust!"

Everyone in the café was listening so intently that they strained forward, waiting for Festus's reply.

"Aw, dagnabbit, I'll do it, Clara."

"I *knew* you wouldn't walk out on me!" she cried,

leaning far across the table and hugging his neck. "And after we get Ted to Texas, I'll divorce him and we'll be married and live ever so happily ever after!"

Festus didn't trust himself to speak. He glanced up from his plate and saw that several of the rough miners were sniffling and completely overcome with emotion.

"Let's eat well," he managed to say, "and then let's go someplace where we can sit down and figure out how best to find your husband."

"All right," she said, beaming. "Oh, thank you!"

And then the worst thing imaginable happened. Some fool prospector with his napkin tucked in his shirtfront and tears in his eyes jumped up and began to applaud. Then others joined him . . . and soon, the entire room was full of clapping fools.

Festus hung his head down and shoveled in his food, feeling his cheeks burn. This sure wasn't the way he'd planned things to go this morning . . . but the truth be known, it was much better.

CHAPTER
23

Festus and Clara traveled through all the Colorado gold camps west of Pikes Peak into the middle of September. At night, they either stayed at a hotel, where Festus slept on the floor beside Clara's bed, ready to protect her honor, or else they rolled up in their blankets and a starlit sky was their celestial ceiling. The trouble was, it rained nearly every day in the high mountains and the nights were already getting cold. They grew dirty, tired, and increasingly miserable, but not once did either of them consider giving up the search for Ted Austin.

Clara had a picture of her husband that she displayed to everyone she met. Sometimes they got a lead on him, but it never panned out, because everyone seemed constantly on the move, running between gold strikes.

But in the third week of September, they finally got a break when the bandy-legged proprietor of a roadside saloon studied Ted's picture, clucked his tongue, and said, "Yes, ma'am, I seen this fella just two days ago."

"Where!" Clara exclaimed.

The saloon keeper was a bearded leprechaun named Mickey Maguire, with a sparkle in his mischievous eyes and very few upper teeth. "Well now, I guess that information appears to be mighty important to you, huh?"

"It sure is," Festus replied. "We've been hunting all over these mountains."

"Is this man wanted for something . . . like murder?" Maguire asked, judging the worth of his information.

"No, he's my husband and it's personal," Clara snapped. "Will you please tell us where you saw him?"

"Hmm, seems to me . . . no, it wasn't there." Maguire scratched his scraggly beard, then gazed down at hands no larger than those of a boy. "I'm just havin' trouble rememberin' right now. Might come to me after a while, though . . . but I don't know."

Festus was the first to catch Maguire's meaning. He dug a rumpled dollar from his pocket but the money was ignored, telling him that the price of this information was not going to come that cheap.

"Here," Clara said, slapping a gold piece on the makeshift bar. "But first you're going to tell me everything I ask."

"Hmm," Mickey Maguire said, a smile bringing dimples to his cherry-red cheeks, "methinks my memory is coming back just now!"

Festus held his tongue. If he were in Dodge City, he'd have jerked the Irishman up short and shook the truth out of him. But this wasn't Dodge and he had no authority, so he ground his teeth in seething silence.

"First," Clara said, "exactly where did you see my husband?"

"Just a couple miles west of here, dealing cards in the Plug Nickel Saloon."

"And where is that?"

"In Dogtown, which is just over this divide."

Festus heard the tremor in Clara's voice. "Are you *sure* this is the right man? Take a very good look at this picture, Mr. Maguire."

"I don't have to, ma'am. It is he!"

Maguire's hand stabbed out for the gold piece, but Festus clamped it to the bar, saying, "If you're lying to us, we'll be back and you'll be sorry."

"Ah now," Maguire cried, managing to look as if his feelings were badly injured, "there's no need for threatenin' a poor old man! I'm telling you the gospel truth, I swear on the grave of my dear mother!"

"All right, then," Festus said, his grip still clamped down tight. "Tell us everything you can about Dogtown and the Plug Nickel Saloon."

"Not much to tell," Maguire replied, fingers crabbing around the gold coin. "Dogtown is a den of thieves, without law or decency. The depravity you will find there is—"

"Never mind that," Clara interrupted, "tell us about the saloon."

"It is the biggest building in Dogtown and is made of brick and wood. There are rooms in the back for . . . well, to put it delicately, the soiled doves. Upstairs there are more rooms for rent, but you must share them with huge cockroaches."

"Is that where my husband is living?"

Maguire shrugged his narrow shoulders. "I cannot say. I did not room with him, but only played cards at his table, and the scoundrel cheated me! I lost three dollars, but kept me mouth shut so I did not lose my poor life."

"How was Ted dressed?" Clara asked.

"About like your friend here, but he was much . . . well . . . bite my tongue, but he was a devilishly handsome rogue. Tall, with good teeth! He wears gold rings on most of his fingers, you understand."

"That's definitely Ted," Clara said firmly. "He loved

gold rings and would often offer to buy them from his winnings."

Maguire nodded as if he already knew this to be true. He grinned at Festus and said, "There now, I'll be having that coin under my hand . . . if you please."

"Let's go," Clara said, already turning to hurry toward the divide.

Festus ran to overtake her and said, "We can't just go barging into the saloon."

"Why not?"

"Well, he's probably gonna have friends and I can't whip them all."

"You won't have to," she replied. "Just let me handle my husband."

"Well, Clara, if you could do that by yourself, why am I here!"

She turned her head sideways at him and said, "Because if he goes crazy and shoots me, I'll at least die knowing that you killed him in return."

"I ain't gonna let him kill you!"

"Good! Now, please be quiet and let me decide what I want to say to him first."

Dogtown was like a dozen other haphazardly thrown-together mining camps they'd seen in the past few weeks. "There's the saloon," Festus said, pointing up the street.

"I'm not feeling well, and I'd like to eat and wash my face before I see Ted."

Festus was hungry, too. They hadn't eaten since early morning and it had been a hard climb over the divide. Clara looked tired; muddy creases lined her drawn face. It occurred to Festus that this poor woman had been under tremendous mental as well as physical strain.

"Look," he said, "there's a café just a couple of doors up the street. Why don't we go in there and you order something while I go over to the Plug Nickel and—"

"No!" She lowered her voice. "If you challenged Ted, he might misunderstand and try to kill you. I have to try and reason with him first. All right?"

"Clara, I can't let you face him alone. Not after what you told me."

Clara opened her mouth to say something, then changed it and nodded in agreement. "If you insist."

"I sure do. You hired me to do a job and it ain't quite finished."

"Thank you, Festus. I don't know what I would do without your strength and courage."

"I'll just go over there and make sure that he hasn't left town," Festus explained. "Then I'll come right back."

"Hurry."

"I will," he promised.

As always, the main street was clotted with freight wagons churning up huge chunks of mud. Picking his way across the street to the saloon, Festus checked the six-gun on his hip, although he would honor Clara's wish and avoid a showdown with Ted Austin. He felt apprehensive about finally meeting this poor excuse for a man and, at the same time, relieved that Clara's ordeal was almost behind them.

"Afternoon," he said to the rotund bartender who came to take his order.

"What can I pour you, stranger?"

"I am looking for Ted Austin."

"I don't know him."

This is going to be rough right to the end, Festus thought, trying to keep from losing his temper.

"He's a gambler. Big, handsome friend of mine with a bunch of gold rings on his fingers. You must know him."

"I don't know nobody," the bartender replied stoically, "and I always mind my own business."

Festus choked back the impulse to grab this man by the shirtfront. Instead, he dug into his pockets and laid five precious dollars on the bar top. "I come a long way to find my friend. I sure would appreciate you givin' this another thought."

The bartender stared at the money, then at Festus. "You a lawman?"

"No."

"All right," he said in a low voice. "You'd find him tonight anyway when he comes down to work the table. Only he don't go by the name of Austin."

"I don't care what name he goes by," Festus said. "Where is he now?"

"Jeb sleeps days; upstairs, second room on the right."

"Thanks. I'm going to eat now, but I'll be back later. And say, don't tell him a friend came asking. Okay?"

"Sure. Don't matter to me what you want to see Jeb about. He's a pretty boy who thinks he's God's gift to women and I can't abide him anyway."

Festus left the saloon. He had to wait a minute for a procession of ore wagons to pass slowly down the street and then he hurried back to tell Clara the news, but she was gone.

"Where is she?" he asked the cook.

"Had to use the privy out back and wanted to wash up a little, so I let her go out through the kitchen. Your food is comin' up."

Festus slumped down at the little table and studied his reflection in the window. He sure wasn't looking very shiny anymore and barely had enough money left for travel expenses back to Dodge City. But at least he was doing the right thing. Clara would never have been able to search these rough mining camps without a good man offering her protection.

"Coffee, mister?"

"Sure," Festus answered.

"You look like you've been down a long, rough road. That lady don't look too good either."

"We're both worn out," Festus snapped with irritation. The last thing he needed right now was idle conversation.

"Food will be right up," the cook told him as he poured two cups and then went back to the kitchen.

Festus sipped his coffee and gazed out the dirty window. Dogtown was sure a busy place and he'd bet that this meal was going to cost them plenty. Well, Clara could pay this time, even if it wasn't very gentlemanly of him to allow it.

"Here you go. Steak and potatoes."

"Thanks," Festus said, glancing anxiously toward the kitchen. "Maybe I better go see if the lady is all right."

"They take longer than a man."

Festus frowned, for it was not proper to speak of such things about a lady. "Just the same, I better check."

"Suit yourself, but pay before you go. Comes to three dollars and ten cents. I can't afford for both of you to maybe duck out on me without gettin' paid."

Festus knew there was no way out of paying. Feeling taken advantage of, he paid the bill and then hurried through the kitchen and out the back door into the alley. He saw the privy and called, "Clara, are you feelin' all right?"

No answer.

"Clara, if you're sick, yell out."

Still no answer.

Good Lord, what if she fainted in the privy or even fell . . . no, that couldn't happen . . . could it?

Festus rushed to the door and knocked. "Clara . . ."

When there still wasn't an answer, he yanked the door open and the privy was empty. Festus swung around in a complete circle. The alley was deserted!

He dashed back into the kitchen, grabbed the cook, and yelled, "Where did she go?"

"How should I know?"

One of the other customers, no doubt seeing Festus's panic and taking pity, called, "If you're lookin' for that pretty lady you brought in, she went across the street and into the Plug Nickel Saloon."

"Oh my gosh!"

Festus burst out the door and was nearly run over by a wagon. He dodged between a mule and a horse, then leaped up the far sidewalk and burst into the Plug Nickel. The bartender he'd spoken to looked up suddenly.

"Did you see a lady go upstairs?"

"A lot of women go upstairs."

"Yeah, but this was a *lady*!"

"I guess I did."

Festus took the stairs two steps at a time, his heart in his throat. Just as he reached the head of the stairs, there was a volley of gunfire. He tore his gun free and went charging down the hallway.

"Clara!"

Clara backed woodenly out of the room, a smoking derringer in her fist and blood coursing down her left arm. Her face was pale and she staggered, but Festus caught her in his arms and eased her to the floor.

"Darling, I'm going to be all right. It's just a scratch. Don't let him get away!"

Festus jumped into the room and crouched with his gun up and ready to fire. He needn't have bothered to hurry because Ted Austin was lying on the floor, lips forming frothy red bubbles caused by a bullet hole in his chest. The man was extremely handsome and he smelled of bay rum and cigars. He was trying desperately to speak; Festus leaned close, but could not make out the words before he expelled his last breath.

Festus rushed back into the hallway. "Clara, why didn't you wait for me?"

"You might have gotten killed. You don't deserve that."

"You danged fool!"

Because it was unlikely that there was a doctor in Dogtown, Festus scooped the woman up and placed her on the bed. "Lay still while I take a look at that wound."

"Is my husband dead?"

"Yep."

"Good!" she hissed between clenched teeth. "Good riddance!"

"But what about all those papers he needed to sign?"

"He doesn't have to sign them if he's proven dead," she whispered as men and women filled the doorway.

"Get out of here!" Festus warned, drawing his gun and pointing it toward the gawkers. "There's nothing left to see."

They vanished. Festus took a deep breath, holstered his gun, and looked down at Clara. "I sure wish that you'd let me help you, but I can't be angry with someone that was trying to protect my life."

"Oh, Festus my darling, I'd do *anything* for you."

Unable to speak because he was so overcome, Festus concentrated on washing and bandaging her arm.

"I'm sorry if I made you mad."

It took Festus a few minutes to trust himself to say, "Nobody other than Matthew, Kitty, and Doc ever stood up for me thataway."

"It's almost over now," she told him, closing her eyes as he finished with her arm, "and I am so tired."

"I'll go find an undertaker and—"

"No," she cried, eyes popping open quickly, "I need to be alone with Ted for a few minutes."

"Why!"

"You have to remember that when I first fell in love, he was a different man. I need to say good-bye in private." She smiled weakly. "You can understand that, can't you?"

"I guess so."

"Did you eat?"

"No. I left our food on the table."

"Then go eat and bring me back something, please."

That made sense to Festus, who had been taught never to waste food or money. "I'll hurry."

"Good, and bring a photographer."

"A what?"

"Because the court back home in Austin will need proof that Ted is dead. Just . . . just please bring a photographer. I'll pay him."

"Okay." Festus leaned over and kissed her lips. "Goodbye, darlin'."

"Good-bye, my heart."

Festus could hardly keep the tears from spilling down his cheeks as he tiptoed out of the room, leaving her to what he sure hoped was a blessed and well-deserved sleep.

CHAPTER

24

"Next station is Dodge City!" the conductor called as he hurried down the aisle. "Passengers bound for Dodge City prepare to depart!"

Festus squeezed Clara's hand and said hopefully, "We could be married right here in Dodge City. I know the preacher and—"

"Darling, I just can't. My daughter is only four, but she'd be so disappointed if we weren't married in Austin with my family. And imagine how pretty she will be as a flower girl."

"All right," Festus agreed, "we'll go down to Texas and get married."

"And I'm sure that you'll be happy living there," Clara told him. "I think you will be the town marshal someday."

Festus blushed. "Aw, now, let's not get way ahead of ourselves. Austin is the capital and—"

"You can do it," Clara vowed. "Together, we'll go a long, long ways."

Festus's chest filled with pride. He could hardly believe how quickly and completely his life was changing. Why, just three months ago he was a lowly deputy wearing dirty old clothes and looking like a hillbilly bumpkin. Now, with his suit cleaned, his boots repolished, and the talc powder on his Stetson still hiding the grime and sweat stains, he was a new man.

"I'm sorry we can't live in Dodge City. I know that you're going to really miss your friends." Clara sighed.

"I sure will. Matthew is the best man I ever worked for. Doc, Kitty, Sam, and some of the other folks have been like my real family these past few years."

"You'll start a new family in Texas," she promised, kissing his cheek.

"I expect that I will."

Festus stared out the window at the familiar surroundings. He had been in West Texas and that wasn't nothin' to brag about. Austin was probably a whole lot finer and he was eager to see the lay of that land.

"Clara, before we left Pueblo, I sent a telegram tellin' Matthew we'd be on this train."

"You did?"

"Sure enough. I hope he's recovered and that he found a good deputy, since I won't be comin' back to take my job."

"So do I," Clara said as the train rolled into the depot and people began to climb out of their seats.

"Look!" Festus called. "There they are—Matthew, Doc, and Kitty! Why, even old Sam the bartender and Percy Crump showed up to greet us."

"How nice."

"Let's go!" Festus said, hardly able to hold down his excitement.

A few minutes later they were all grinning, hugging, and slapping each other on the back. One man stood apart and it wasn't until they were ready to leave that Matthew said, "Festus, this is Wolf. He's been my deputy since you've been gone."

Festus was surprised, because Wolf was obviously a half-breed, but he liked the look of the quiet, handsome young man. There was a reserved quality about Wolf that said more than any words that he was not a man to be crossed or insulted.

"Festus," Wolf offered, "welcome back."

"Thanks! I hope Matthew hasn't been treatin' you too bad," Festus joked.

"He hasn't. But I'm ready to move on. I'm not cut out to wear a lawman's badge."

The grin on Festus's face died. He started to tell them that he wasn't going to be able to take back his old job, then changed his mind, deciding that this was neither the time nor the place to make this troubling announcement.

"We'll marry soon and live in Austin," Clara told everyone. "So we won't be able to visit with you more than a few days."

This time it was Matthew's smile that slipped. But he recovered and shook Festus's hand, saying, "Congratulations."

"Yeah," Doc said without enthusiasm. "It's nice to know that you're finally going to settle down and take some *real* responsibility."

"Wolf," Matthew said, turning to his deputy, "I hope you'll stick with me long enough to find your replacement . . . though that won't be easy."

"I won't leave you in a fix," Wolf told him.

The conversation then turned to the Colorado adventure that Festus and Clara had just survived. That carried them back into Dodge and ended with Festus saying, "I almost lost Clara in a Dogtown saloon when she slipped away from me and shot it out with her husband."

Matthew turned to Clara, studying her closely. "You shot and killed him?"

"Look at my arm," she told him, showing off the bandage. "I had to kill Ted, or he would have killed me first!"

"She's lucky to be alive," Festus proudly told everyone.

"She sure is," Matthew said. "Festus, why don't you come by and we'll catch up on things after you and Clara settle in at the Dodge House?"

"I'll do it, Matthew. So long, Wolf."

Wolf nodded gravely. Then Doc and Kitty were telling them to come on over to the Long Branch Saloon after dinner for a few beers.

"We'll be there," Festus promised.

It was an hour later before Festus could break free and go visit his best friend Matthew. He was feeling kind of sad and nostalgic about the good life he'd had in Dodge and how much he was going to miss it and his friends.

"Festus," Matt said in greeting, "things are sure happening fast for you."

"I can't believe I got so lucky."

"And lucky for Clara, too."

"I swear I don't know why Clara went and done such a crazy thing. She said—"

"Maybe I can tell you why she shot her husband," Matthew interrupted.

"Huh?"

"Look at this," Matthew told him, extending a telegram.

"What . . . "

"Festus, it's from a Marshal J. T. Judd in Austin, Texas. I contacted him just after you left for Colorado. Maybe you'd better sit down before you start reading."

Festus glanced at Wolf, who quickly looked away. He picked up the telegram and began to read.

Dear Marshal Dillon:

Regarding your request for information on Ted Austin and Clara Austin. Based on your description and the facts that I have at hand, I can tell you that neither of these persons is related to Stephen Austin or the Austin family of Austin, Texas.

"Ted" Austin is an alias for Doug Hirt, a notorious thief and gambler. Based on your description of Clara Austin, she can be no other than Mrs. Sarah Hirt, a woman of very questionable background and morals who is suspected to have joined her outlaw husband in several bank and stage robberies. Unfortunately, as there are no living witnesses to these robberies, we cannot issue a warrant for the arrest of Mrs. Hirt. I can tell you she has a four-year-old daughter named Mary, being raised by her grandparents, who have no wish to ever see the young woman again.

Doug Hirt is a thief and killer who is wanted dead or alive. There is a one-thousand-dollar bounty on his carcass, payable upon delivery of his body or proof of death here in Austin, Texas. Hope this answers some of your questions, and thanks for keeping the lid on things when our cowboys come to enjoy your hospitality.

Sincerely,
J. T. Judd
Marshal of Austin, Texas

Matt shook his head and expelled a deep breath, "Festus, I'm awful sorry to give you this news. I hated the thought of losing you, but Wolf and I decided we had to tell you the truth about Sarah Hirt just as soon as possible."

"She's a pretty woman," Wolf said, "but . . . to put it like an Indian, she speaks with forked tongue."

"Yeah." Festus pushed himself to his feet. "I guess I won't be going to Texas after all."

"Maybe I will," Wolf said quietly.

Both Matthew and Festus looked at the deputy with a question in their eyes.

"Like I said," Wolf told them with a shrug of his shoulders. "She *is* a pretty woman and I got a feeling that she's going to have some problems collecting and then spending that thousand reward. Festus, after all the lies you've heard, do you still want to marry or help her?"

"No," Festus heard himself say.

"Then there's no reason I shouldn't," Wolf said, unpinning his badge, walking over, and giving it back to Festus.

When Wolf reached the door, he turned and said, "Marshal, it's been an education. Good luck!"

"Thanks," Matt said, eyes glued on poor Festus.

"Deputy?"

Festus looked up at the half-breed, who told him, "I'm sorry it worked out like this but you are lucky you didn't marry her, 'cause she'll never be the kind you can trust."

"Maybe I should at least go—"

"No. You don't owe her a damn thing," Wolf told him. "She owes *you*."

"He's right," Matt said. "I'm just sorry I can't arrest and toss her in jail."

"I'm not," Festus said in a small voice.

Wolf and Clara or Sarah left the very next morning and Festus never told the woman good-bye. Soon after the train departed, Kitty and Doc found him sitting beside the Arkansas River, skipping stones.

"Festus," Kitty said, "Sarah left you something."

"What?"

"The wedding ring. She said you'd find a better woman someday, marry her and become a marshal."

"I don't want it."

"Aw, for cripes sakes, go on and take it!" Doc growled. "Those were the only true words that Texas woman ever uttered!"

Festus couldn't bear even to look at the ring and he didn't open its box before slipping it into his pocket.

"Your heartache will pass," Kitty promised. "In time it will pass."

Festus tried but failed to smile. "I don't know about that, Miss Kitty. Clara made me feel awful tall."

"That's not a bit true," Kitty argued. "You were feeling tall, proud, and handsome weeks before she arrived in Dodge City. Don't you remember?"

"No, I do not."

"Well, you were," she assured him. Then, looking up at Doc, Kitty said, "Uncork the bottle. We've got some remembering to do and some sad love stories to share."

"Damn right we do," Doc grumped, sitting on the other side of Festus. "How many times you already got a rock to skip?"

"Only three."

"Well," Doc mused, "before this whiskey is all gone, we'll *all* manage to do a lot better!"

Kitty rested her arm across Festus's shoulders. "It might help to remember you're going to stay with your best friends."

Festus took the bottle from Doc, drank deeply, and then managed to whisper loud enough for them to hear, "Yes, Miss Kitty, I expect it'll help aplenty."